CALABASH

STORIES

CALABASH

STORIES

JEFFREY J. HIGA

PLEIADES
P R E S S

ROBERT C. JONES PRIZE SERIES
WARRENSBURG, MISSOURI

Published by Pleiades Press

Department of English
University of Central Missouri
Warrensburg, Missouri 64093

Distributed by Louisiana State University Press

Cover Art: Edwin Ushiro

Book design by David Wojciechowski

First Pleiades Printing, 2021

Financial support for this project has been provided by the University of Central Missouri, as well as the Missouri Arts Council, the Missouri Humanities Council. and the Literary Arts Emergency Fund.

For my grandmother, Grace Umeko Matsuyoshi, who taught me to believe.

And for my daughter, Raine Eun Joo Umeko Kamalei Higa, may she carry on the belief.

CONTENTS

THE SHADOW ARTIST

The Shadow Artist knew himself to be a relic. A walking anachronism in the forgotten uniform of his profession: the black top hat, the formal doublet and waistcoat, the black bowtie. He knew the cartoonish figure he cut, a wandering aristocrat dragged from the previous century, traveling the red dirt roads from sugar plantation to sugar plantation in West Oahu. And yet, all of this—his clothing, his art, his manner—he assumed with a solemnity bordering on the sacred, as if his very existence were some kind of offering to a deity long discredited. This reverence silenced those who might ridicule him, and instead, they looked on in silent curiosity, stopped in the midst of their activities, waiting for him to pass before restarting the sweep of their lives.

He had once made his rounds in the cooling heights of Mānoa, received at front doors and ushered into homes with the fuss due a visiting regent. Girls would don their finest dresses, mothers would slick back the hair of their unruly sons, even fathers would venture down in their Sunday best for a session with the Shadow Artist. He had used the finest French papers then, *blanc et noir*, ordered from a distributor in Tahiti, and after hanging the white sheets behind his subject, he would create shadow profiles from whatever illumination was available: candle, gas lamp, and later, electricity. He would then sit with the subject and talk with him or her for nearly an hour as he cut constantly, reducing the white life-sized outlines smaller and smaller until the very last minute, when he slipped a black sheet under the white and cut the final portrait. In this way he had been different from his colleagues, competitors who boasted of their speed—"Portraits cut in under ten seconds! Families in under a minute!"—and relied on their flashing scissors and scraps of flying black paper for their drama. The Shadow Artist relied on the subtle drama of transformation, the movement from rough outlines to definitive portraits, from working white to final black. He allowed his subjects to talk about themselves, their words shaping changes to a line here, a minimizing of features there, until he revealed to them the silhouette that they themselves had always desired.

His colleagues had ridiculed him for it, for in their time, they could make more in fifteen minutes than he could make in a day, but here, now, it was this difference that made him the last. He watched them get squeezed out of the piers where the cruise ships docked, and replaced on the downtown street corners by dabblers in what would come to be known as photography. At first, the Shadow Artist believed that there would always be a place for his skills beside this new dirty science with its arcane processes, stinking chemicals, and exploding elements. But people seemed to clamor for these frozen moments of time, these portraits of merciless detail, so unlike his timeless silhouettes with details combed and edited over with an eye to eternity.

Now all he had left were his weekly appointments at the plantation death houses in the sugarcane fields of West Oahu. These sojourns, another relic from earlier times, were at the behest of the Japanese and Filipino labor unions who paid him a small remuneration for capturing the likenesses and personal histories of their valetudinary members. He mailed this information once a week to the unions, where, eventually, the information would be used in the obituary sections of the Filipino- and Japanese-language newspapers. The Shadow Artist did not know why he was still on the union payroll—even the newspapers would not print silhouettes anymore—but he figured that he was being tolerated out of pity, not unlike the pity shown to the residents of the death houses. These unmarried, family-less men who had worked themselves until they broke and had lost all of their money to whoring, gambling, and foolish investments had nowhere else to go and lived out the remainder of their lives in the communal charity of the death houses. As a younger man, the Shadow Artist had contemplated the death houses with a kind of superstitious dread, but now, nearly the same age as these residents, he approached them with almost an obscene comfort as the final witness to these men whispering out their lives without notice—a fitting metaphor, he felt, for how he and his art would go.

The death houses were easy to find. They were always located early on the main road into the plantation and were always the solitary structures near the cemeteries across the road from the main plantation camps. Even death could not deny blood, and so there were usually two death houses: one that served the Filipino camp and another for the Japanese camp. Here, stuck between the living and the dead—the sounds of life emanating from the plantation camp in front of them, and the silence of the burial ground on the other—the Shadow Artist first learned of the strike.

"You never hear?" the old Japanese man asked. "The Filipinos strike yesterday all over Oahu. Strike leader Manlapit went call for it."

The Shadow Artist said nothing for a moment as he continued to cut the old man's profile, sharpening the jaw line. "And the Japanese? What?"

"Nothing. Working still. Meeting every night, 'We going? We no going?'" The old man shook his head disgustedly. "Some still mad from last time we strike and the planters stop hiring Japanese."

The Shadow Artist nodded and slipped in a black sheet under the white. "They went bring in the Filipinos then…"

"Yeah, the planters come scared. Try bring in another race and reduce our numbers." The old man shifted in his bed. "If I still had my back, I'd go tell 'em we not divided by race. We divided by money. The Filipinos and Japanese stay standing next to the others looking up the hill at the *haoles*."

"All *pau*." The Shadow Artist passed the black silhouette over to the old man and slipped the white copy into the pages of a thick book that he always carried with him. He had made the book himself so long ago that the black paper of its pages was turning gray on the edges. It contained a white copy of every profile he had ever cut. Its heft comforted him during the long and lonely treks between plantations, for, in its earlier pages, it was heavy with the history and likenesses of some of the most powerful families on the island.

"Try look," the old man smiled at his profile. "Still strong, eh?"

The Shadow Artist nodded. "It's your shoulders…"

The old man handed the silhouette back to the Shadow Artist. "No, it's you. I know I not going die that way."

The Shadow Artist rolled the black profile in with his notes about the old man. "But the Federation of Labor will remember you that way."

The old man shrugged and turned toward the window. He studied his clear view of the cemetery: the skewed and scattered volcanic rocks serving as crude headstones, even the recent ones already chipping away, erasing the names of the dead; the cane grass, knee high and undisturbed, threatening to engulf the stones while providing homes for the rodents and mongooses, the only living things that ever frequented this area. "No," he said, "no one has time to remember."

Everywhere the Shadow Artist went in the Filipino camp, everyone asked him the same thing: What's wrong with the Japanese? Why do they still go to work? They're unreliable, aren't they? There's a dishonest race that crosses our picket lines. All the Shadow Artist could do was shrug his shoulders and continue to make his way toward the death house. He was surprised that despite the hundreds of men and women just milling about, the camp was quiet, and he could feel their eyes upon him, searching him for answers he did not bring.

So it was with a certain relief that he could duck into the death house to deal with matters that he knew intimately: dignity and the dying. During the week since his last visit, two of the residents had died, and so the Shadow Artist recorded their bango numbers for the Filipino newspaper. These numbers replaced a person's name in the plantation rolls, and only those whose station was above—the *lunas*, overseers, field bosses, and planters—were addressed by name. Everyone else was given a number on a tin tag to be carried with them like branded chattel. The Shadow Artist always waited until the men died before learning and recording their bango numbers. He wanted these men to know that what would follow them after death was not their number, but the only thing they had left, their name.

Sitting down with the two new replacement residents, however, the Shadow Artist did little cutting. These men, unburdened by retirement, could still remember the yoke of the plantation system and spoke of nothing but the strike. They spoke to the Shadow Artist like a fellow laborer, as if he had shared with them the long hours in the sun, felt the fear of the *luna*'s black snake whip, and obeyed the whistle that regimented all aspects of their day from rising in the morning to lights out at night. He understood that it was not their shared toil that mattered so much to these men as it was his willingness to look backward with them, to revive a past that mattered little to an immigrant population looking only to strive forward. The Shadow Artist thought that the only recompense he could offer these men who had yielded up a lifetime of confidences to him was to capture their profiles at this moment of truth, their last long moment of looking back before facing the inevitable that awaited them.

But sitting with those men in the death house that day, talking not of the past but of the present, reaching not to superstition but to the future by keeping open the outside door to welcome whatever developments may come, the Shadow Artist could feel a strange welling, like a surge of blood, inside himself. A sudden warmth pervaded his body and he stood, compelled by a rush he had experienced only once before: the first time he ever saw a master perform the art that would eventually consume the Shadow Artist. It was an emotion as clear as a call to arms and as real to him as a push, a feeling he equated with his destiny.

"I must leave," he told his startled audience. When they asked why, all he could say was, "To complete my own shadow."

By the next day, Pinkerton agents had been brought onto the plantations to bolster the plantation police forces. Armed with rifles, shotguns, and clubs of various kinds, the Pinkertons prevented the Filipino laborers from forming picket lines near the Japanese camps and enforced a strict separation between the two. Camp after camp, the Shadow Artist was stopped by these roughnecks, questioned, and searched. He told them the truth, that he was there to record the likenesses and words of the dying and that unless they were ready to wrest the kitchen knives out of the hands of every wife and mother on the plantation, his scissors were no threat to them. Scorning his delicate manners, and amused by his foppish appearance and impotent mission, the agents always let him pass, as if he were a harmless old woman.

It was then that the Shadow Artist's real work began. Though he would enter through the death houses, he was not there to speak to the residents. He might start with them, turning occasionally to a passerby in the open doorway, telling of his long trips between the sugar plantations of West Oahu, and of the things he had seen and heard: the plantation police arming themselves, the Pinkerton agents with their beards and long guns, rumors that the Hawaiian Sugar Planters' Association were bringing in special strike breakers from the mainland, men who specialized in "breaking down" union loyalty and strike leaders. Working slowly, as he always did, he would trim shapes out of the edges of his black paper—a wooly Pinkerton profile, a menacing gun, a caricature of a major sugar planter—leaving the middle of the sheet untouched until he had generated a small audience of onlookers and the curious.

He would turn to the audience then, and begin, "There are spies everywhere, so what I tell you should not be repeated…" thereby ensuring propagation through the illicit thrill in the retelling. He started with the head, telling his audience of the man he had seen, "a *hanahana* worker, like yourselves," giving neither name nor ethnicity, relying instead on the anonymity of the profile he cut to let his Filipino or Japanese audiences draw their own conclusions. For safety's sake he could not tell them exactly which plantation this man was from, the Shadow Artist said as he cut the steep crags of the Ko'olau Mountains into the background, but he was living in another camp "just down the *mauka* side." The Shadow Artist finished the countenance with an open mouth, for it was the man's words and ideas that were most important. He talked of Japanese and Filipino workers standing "shoulder to shoulder," and while he cut a strong arm ending in a fist, he explained how they had reached beyond blood to grasp their futures away from the ruling races. "We call ourselves Chinese, Portuguese, Swedish, Japanese, Koreans, or Filipino," he said as black scraps fell away in the shapes of these mother countries, "but our hearts and our bellies are here in these islands."

"He knows that we have all come for the same thing," he said as he cut into the profile the outline of a ship. "The opportunity to work, to make our lives better." With a few cuts, the peaks of the ship were transformed into waves of standing sugar cane. "Does the cane care who cuts it?"

The Shadow Artist paused for a reply. When there was none, he held up the black silhouette of the cane field. "I said, does the cane care who cuts it?"

"No," came a mumbled reply.

"No, of course not," said the Shadow Artist and he dramatically snipped off the bottom half of the cane field and rotated the paper to reveal a profile of a man, unmistakably a planter in a plantation hat, the slope of his nose cut in the peculiar Roman angles that seemed extreme to his audience and bespoke only one race, haole. "Even the planters don't care who cuts it—Japanese, Filipino, Chinese, or whatever."

A murmur of assent grew among the crowd.

"He asks us, if the planters don't care who does the work, then why should it matter to the workers themselves?" The Shadow Artist paused to resurrect the arm punctuated by a fist, this time on a smaller scale. "The planters value nothing but our labor; let them tremble at its withholding!"

At this point, the crowd became more vocal, but the Shadow Artist did not hear them. He busily cut the profile of the crowd itself before the upheld fist. "Let us sever the chains of King Sugar," he continued as he shaped the body silhouette of a man in front of the crowd, "So that a wage increase for one is a wage increase for all!"

The crowd roared. The Shadow Artist raised up his completed profile, a shade of a man leading all gathered before him to the land of wild promise that these men remembered leaving their homes, their families, and their histories for. "Men of all countries, unite! We have but these islands to win!"

The Shadow Artist stepped back before someone grabbed the silhouette from his fingers and held it aloft to the cheering crowd. Even the scraps—pieces of cane, outlines of countries and guns, broken profiles—were grabbed up and passed around like holy relics of a wondrous event. The Shadow Artist watched the crowd turn from him and disperse like a wave out the door and onto the street, before he himself turned to slip out the back door to journey on to the next plantation.

As the planters and the Pinkertons tightened their grip on the plantation camps on Oahu, the Shadow Artist continued to move between them unmolested. At each camp, he stopped in the death houses to tell the story of this unnamed strike leader, adding more details every time—a little more history just remembered, a line added to the speeches, a new personal affectation he could cut—further solidifying the profile. Sometimes, he would become confused and find himself telling the audiences his own story, about his dreams and his failures and the illusions that shielded him, that shielded all of them before that moment he discovered the strike leader. By week's end, the Shadow Artist had audiences waiting for him in the death houses who were already well informed on the strike leader through the uncontainable human grapevine that nurtured the plantations. He found these audiences repeating the popular parts of story lines with him verbatim, and occasionally having his words confirmed by an audience member who claimed to have met the strike leader or been at an event. In this way, the Shadow Artist wove the plantations together into a net of solidarity that went unnoticed by the planters and its informers until too late. A week after the Filipinos first struck for higher wages, the Japanese joined them in what would come to be known as the Great Strike.

Reaction by the Hawaiian Sugar Planters' Association was swift. They immediately condemned the strike as illegal and a threat to the national security of the territory. "Hawaii's economy is being held hostage by a few rabble-rousers out for their own gain," wrote the main English-language daily, urging the planters to speed up importation of new races. By controlling the banks, the HSPA was able to pressure financially strapped Filipino- and Japanese-language newspapers into denouncing the strike and its leaders, albeit in weak and watered-down prose. Secretly, the HSPA called for a meeting with this "so-called unnamed strike leader" to determine if he could be bought, and if not, the bounty to put on his head. As a final insult, the plantations issued evictions to all striking workers from the camps, forcing tens of thousands of Filipino and Japanese laborers to migrate from rural Oahu to Honolulu where the labor unions provided free meals to strikers.

The Shadow Artist, however, continued to attend to the death houses even though his weekly remittances from the labor unions had stopped as soon as the strike began. His body had long been animated by habit rather than reason, and so he found himself climbing the worn death house stairs to assist in the evacuation of the residents. He readied them for the road while the Pinkerton agents thumped their clubs on the floor or along the halls while they waited impatiently to close up the houses. The young and strong had left days ago, and so on the roads, the Shadow Artist met only the elderly and infirm in a parade of broken humanity shambling past him, all headed in the same direction, as if on their way to a faith healer.

Occasionally one of these residents would stop him to tell him the latest news—the Koreans, Hawaiians, and Puerto Ricans had decided not to strike, the planters were offering strike wages over twice the usual plus bonus—or to ask about the strike leader.

"They say he is lying low," he always told them, "or maybe he's on an outer island. Some say he went over there to escape and some say to talk strike with those plantations."

"What do you say?" they would ask him.

"A man can't hide from his destiny," he told them.

It was on the road that several people stopped to tell him that they heard that the Filipinos on the Waialua Plantation were planning to return to work. Their local leader, a man named Llacuna, had suddenly called off the strike, labeling it an "imperialist Japanese plot," and was ordering his people back to work. The strikers in town were surprised and ignored Llacuna, but rumor had it that he was already back at the plantation under the protection of the Pinkertons and recruiting new workers.

The road to Waialua Plantation was long and the Shadow Artist met no one along the way save for a solitary old man who was resting by the side of the road on his trek to Honolulu.

"No, I no hear that," he said. "But I seen plenty new people at the plantation now."

"What kind of people?"

"*Haole*. The kind never stay in the islands long, 'cause still white as rice yet," he said.

"You seen Llacuna with them?" the Shadow Artist asked.

The old man shook his head. "I no like the looks of those new guys, so I leave."

The Shadow Artist nodded and watched the old man gather his belongings and move off. "Hoo, if I could walk to Japan like this," he heard the old man say to himself, "I'd have stay gone long ago."

By the time the Shadow Artist arrived at the main road into the Waialua Plantation, it was just after twilight, and darkness was sliding down the mountains and pooling in the valley quickly. As he made his way to the Filipino death house, he noticed that the old man was right. The plantation police who had waved him onto the plantation a week earlier had been replaced by these beefier thugs who silently watched him with the unblinking eyes of predators, their only movements a ratcheting of their jaws as they chewed tobacco and hissed spit as thick and dark as blood.

The death house was as quiet as a tomb when the Shadow Artist let himself in. He stood a moment to breathe in the stale air and allow his eyes to get used to the darkness. He saw that the house was empty and abandoned, like a dried-up artifact of an extinct civilization. The Shadow Artist's footfalls knocked like pleas down the empty hallways.

"Hello," he called.

The Shadow Artist heard only his own echo before there was a scraping noise and a muffled, "In here…"

"What?" The voice seemed to come from a back room at the end of the hallway. "Hello, Llacuna?"

There was no reply so the Shadow Artist stopped. The silence reigned for a few moments before there was another muffled "In here."

As the Shadow Artist pushed open the door to the room, the stink like an animal weeklong in death rose to greet him. A bright rectangle of yellow light from a nearby window lay distorted and angular on the floor, quivering as clouds passed like apparitions through the streaming moonlight. On either side of the light, standing like demon sentries, stood two bulky roughnecks, their clubs hanging down beside them like natural extensions of their arms. The Shadow Artist felt himself being jerked out of the doorway and the bag torn from his shoulder as the door whistled past his ear and shut.

"So you're…" said a voice over his right shoulder.

"I'm the Shadow Artist," he said and turned to meet that voice when he was suddenly struck behind the knees. Pain shot up his legs as they cracked like a tree branch. He collapsed to the floor, his worthless legs splayed in front of him, convulsing like dying fish.

"We don't really care who you are," said the voice over him. "Who is this?"

The familiar silhouette of the strike leader was thrust into the Shadow Artist's face. He smiled and took the piece of black paper and ran his finger over the profile. I can still repair this edge, he thought and reached into his pocket for his scissors.

"Oh no, you don't," another voice said, and the Shadow Artist felt some-one yank on his arm, forcing his hand to fly out of his pocket. The scissors were wrenched out of his hand and he turned his head to watch the heel of a boot snap his fingers like pencils, the noise and pain of it bringing a smile to his face.

He watched them empty his bag, turning over his heavy book of silhouettes and shaking them out of the pages, a lifetime's worth of white paper flashing in the moonlight momentarily like brilliant memories before sinking into the inky darkness.

"Where can we find him?" the voice demanded.

The Shadow Artist tried to turn his head but found he couldn't. With his good hand still gripping the silhouette, he brought it close to his face and then stuffed it into his mouth. Almost immediately they were upon him, and as they beat and kicked him everywhere, the Shadow Artist lay there and welcomed their blows, his heart bursting with happiness as he waited for that final grace to deliver him into blackness.

CHRISTMAS STORIES

My father spoke of the Hakalau Sugar Plantation like he spoke of death—something immutable that taunted him at every risky venture, greeted him at the end of every failure, and loomed like a buzzard over him, waiting for him to stumble so that it could pick his bones. Having grown up in the Japanese section of the plantation camps, I was used to this kind of traditional morbidity, but my father's fatalism was different. He embellished his specters, animating them and seizing my imagination so securely that I continue to dream of death not as a rattling skeleton, but as a hided cane worker, sweating flesh and dirt, his square, hammertoed feet leaving bloody tracks on the porches and floors of my nightmares. We thought of the plantation as part of our family, a wicked stepfather, perhaps, someplace we could always go back to but without our self-respect. So, in January of 1923, when we left the plantation for the third time, we had no way of knowing for sure that it would be for good.

My parents moved into the Palama area of Oahu, an area filled with Filipino and Japanese plantation expatriates, people like ourselves who possessed the immigrant's vision, like a blindered horse, of only looking forward. My father used to say that he didn't have time to look where we were, only where we were going. It would be many years before I realized this was because where we came from was too deeply inscribed upon his memory. But for me, away from the plantation, a whole world had opened up. Luxuries that I had only heard about and never believed, such as children's shoes, suddenly entered my life, and all things seemed possible.

As his own boss, my father worked harder than ever, keeping the hours of his cane working days, sunrise till sunset, six days a week. He worked as a "yard boy"—cut the grass, trimmed the hedges, tended the flowers. They're called gardeners now, but yard boy is what the *haoles* called it and to call it anything else would have been useless. He prided himself on being quiet and efficient, keeping immaculate flower beds and rarely chatting with the other domestic staff. I imagine the wealthy families in Mānoa that he worked for thought well of him, "a credit to his race," passing his name along to their friends, speaking of his reliability and industry. What they never discovered were his little acts of defiance: our eggplant vines growing amidst their hibiscus groves, the rose gardens he would let die and blame on the insects and later replace with tropical plants, the ponds he created upon request, never warning them about the mosquito breeding.

As the oldest son, I helped him in November and December, so that he could charge a little bit more and try to pay off all our debts before the new year. I helped him for years, happily abandoning my schooling during those two months, eager in the promise of more "firsts"—our first radio, first icebox, first automobile, first house—which was the real measuring stick of our lives. My father's plans, however, were different, as he secretly squirreled away most of the money in the bank, waiting for that day when he could purchase us an entirely new life overnight, that first foothold in the American Dream.

So that December of 1923, we were working the grounds of the VanHarding estate in upper Mānoa. It was the biggest place he worked for and he usually spent his Saturdays there, preparing the grounds for some kind of gala event: the welcoming of a new industrial pioneer to the islands or the hosting of a private charity. I liked working with him on Saturdays; it meant missing Japanese school, but mostly I enjoyed the bus ride from the fevered alleyways of our dusty community up into the cooler reaches of the Ko'olau Mountains and into the shaded valleys of breadfruit and banyan trees. Once there, I was never very much help, just followed him around with the rake or rubbish bag, picked up fallen palm fronds, or watered the hibiscus. But I liked to go with him because sometimes I got near enough to the VanHarding house to catch a glimpse of the inside.

My mother used to call it the *ichiban* white house, because although the other *haole* families had white houses, the VanHarding house was the biggest, the whitest, and the cleanest. My father, however, had another name for it: the *obake* house—ghost house. "Too white," he would say. "No more anybody there during the day. Just like one ghost house." Shaking his head, he would go on, "Why anybody want a white house in the first place? So unnatural, like that. And hard for take care, every time chip and gotta repaint." He would conclude by spreading his arms and saying, "More better have one house like this. If little bit chip, little bit dirty, no matter. Brown paint anyway." Every time he said that I would look at our house and think how poor it looked next to the VanHardings', like newsprint next to linen, and I would hunger even more for what I thought cleanliness and whiteness could buy: prosperity and satisfaction.

That Saturday, as my father piled bananas on top of me while I made a basket with my shirt, I planned my approach to the white house. I would have to run and stay out of sight until the last minute, because if I walked or crossed the open lawn too early, Otsu-san the maid would see me coming and meet me outside the kitchen door. But if I ran and knocked on the door, sometimes Mrs. VanHarding would answer and let me into the kitchen. This time I got lucky.

"Oh, it's the yard boy's son," Mrs. VanHarding said as she held the door open. "Come in."

"Okay," I said. My father would have wanted me to say "thank you," but at that age, I was polite only to people who scared me, like my father and his friends. It never occurred to me to be scared of Mrs. VanHarding. She was one of those *haole* ladies with a big bust, but the dresses she wore made her look soft, like an overstuffed futon pinched too tightly in the middle. Her dresses were fringed in layers of white lace, more lace, I imagined, than in all the dry goods shops on King Street. And she was always powdered and perfumed, even for just staying at home. As she took the bunches from me, I stood close to her and inhaled, and I was instantly transported to the plumeria tree in our yard, wet with dew and still riffling in the morning breeze. It was an intoxicating but soothing fragrance, and once I was there, I didn't want to be anywhere else.

After she finished unloading me, she pulled two bananas from the bunch and offered one to me. "Banana?"

"Okay," I said and then remembered. "Thank you."

We both ate standing up. It was part of the ritual. When she was done, she stepped back and looked at me. "Good?" she asked. "The bananas, I mean?"

I shrugged. Big bananas were okay eating, but they couldn't compare to the sweeter and smaller apple bananas that I stole from our Filipino neighbors. "Anything else?" I asked. My father instructed me that anytime Mrs. VanHarding told me to do something, I was to ask if there was anything more I could do.

"How is your mother?"

I then gave her the answer my mother told me to say whenever the *haole* ladies asked about her. "My mother is good and thanks you for your generosity to our family."

Mrs. VanHarding smiled at me and looked as if she wanted to say something else. In all previous encounters, nothing ever came out. Usually, a minute of silence would pass where she looked around the kitchen nervously, and I would inch closer to smell her better. "Well, goodbye," she would say, and I would say bye, and walk out the door. The ritual complete.

This day, however, in the middle of my sniffing, she said, "Stand up straight."

"Hahh?"

"Stand up straight," she said, as she walked around me and looked. The smell of plumeria had completely surrounded me. "You are eight?"

"Ten," I corrected, which I was, although I felt as if I were lying. "Ten, missus."

"Yes, of course." She stood in front of me again, nodding her head. Her lips were a thin line as she looked me over, top to bottom. "Of course." She looked over her shoulder into the heart of the house, and then turned back to me. "Do not move. I will be right back." And she left the kitchen.

I didn't know what to do. My instincts told me to leave because good surprises rarely came from my father's employers. Extra hours, pay reductions, reprimands, and odious tasks were the kind of surprises I was used to. But I also knew that if I disobeyed Mrs. VanHarding and my father found out, I would be lucky to live the night. Even if I did manage to survive, I could foresee a long week of lectures on responsibility and the precariousness of our financial situation, punctuated by additional emphatic physical reminders. It seemed I had but one choice, so in the few minutes she was gone, I tried not to move. Soon I saw her coming toward me, but I still did not move until she handed me a brown paper bundle wrapped in string.

"Here," she said, "I think these will fit you."

The bundle was soft and I turned it over, but I couldn't see what was in it. I looked up at her and wanted to say something, but I didn't know the proper thing to say. No *haole* lady had ever given a gift to me before. I could only think of what my mother would have said. "Thank you for your generosity to our family."

"I have a son who is your age," she said. "He outgrew these a few years ago, and they were just taking up space in his wardrobe, so I thought…" she paused and looked around the kitchen and then at me again. "Well, your mother might have to alter them a bit."

"Thank you," I said and bowed like my father did when he got paid. "Thank you for your generosity to our family."

"Don't get them dirty when you get outside."

I nodded, bowed again, and ran out the kitchen door, across the lawn, and into the banana grove. "Look," I said to my father as I held up the bundle. "Look at what she gave me!"

"Who?" he asked.

"The *haole* lady," I said, "Mrs. VanHarding. She said she also had a son who was ten and that he didn't need these anymore because they too small for him now and…"

"Gimme that!" he said as he dropped his sickle to the ground and threw off his gloves. He wiped his hands on his shirt and snatched the bundle from my arms. "Why you accept this? We taught you better than that!"

"But… but she said she didn't need these. And I thanked her for it. I did. I said, 'Thank you for…'"

"No." He shook his head. "No charity. We no can accept this."

"But how do you know?" I knew my father would give the bundle back without even opening it. "She said they were too small for him. She said they were just sitting around. They're probably only *boro-boros* anyway…"

My father turned to me with a glare that stilled the rest of my thoughts. "Don't say stupid things, Ma-chan. Put away all our stuff. I going take this back." He turned around and walked towards the house.

I didn't try to stop him. I picked up the sickle and gloves. I knew there was no sense even hoping that he would change his mind. He couldn't accept the gift for some Japanese reason, and I knew from past experience that it was useless to try and convince my father out of his Japanese reasons. I just had to accept them.

Even now, I don't know if he could have explained his "Japanese reasons" to me anyway. In times of uncertainty, these traditions, rooted in his custom and history, were the springs he touched upon to propel all of us into our new future. It was a way I could never fully embrace and I would have to create a new way, balancing the forces of my past with those of my future.

After I finished putting the sickle, gloves, and ladder in the shed behind the white house, I started toward the kitchen door, knowing that my father would wait there, hat in hand, for Mrs. VanHarding to pay him. When I got to the door, my father was still trying to give the bundle back to Mrs. VanHarding, who was shaking her head furiously.

"No," she said. "Please take it. These are just old clothes. I must insist you take it."

"No. Too generous. We no deserve such kindness."

"No. This is not a gift. Walter has outgrown these clothes."

"Then please take the cost out from here," Dad held out the weekly salary Mrs. VanHarding had just given him. "To pay."

"No!" A horrified Mrs. VanHarding looked at me for help. I shrugged. She couldn't win. "Please take them," she repeated.

"No charity," he said. "Not right."

"Yes," she said. "It is right." She took the bundle from my father and thrust it at me. "Anyway, I was giving them to your son. Doesn't he want them?" She turned to look at me. "Don't you want them?"

I couldn't believe that she was trying to get around my father. I knew that if she had not been a woman and also *haole*, he would have been very insulted and left. Instead, he turned toward me and I could see the violence brewing in his eyes: I better not even raise my arms to accept the bundle—or else. But the look on Mrs. VanHarding's face was equally clear: She was not used to being disobeyed, and I was to take the bundle from her. It was up to me to do the right thing, and for the second time that day, I tried not to move.

"It would make my son very happy," she said to my father, "if your son would accept this gift from Walter."

I almost laughed then, thinking, that's not going to work. You have to think of something better than that. But when I turned to look at my father, he had turned away from Mrs. VanHarding and was looking at the ground. He seemed suddenly bashful, something I had rarely seen, and after looking at his shoes for a few seconds, he lifted his head and asked, "How your son? Good, yes?"

She nodded her head but said, "No." And then added quietly, "The doctors say this might be his last Christmas."

My father looked back down at his shoes and then turned to look at me. "My son," he said as he nodded at me, "honored by gift from your son."

I stepped forward and then the bundle was in my arms.

The following Sunday and the entire rest of the week was frantic as my parents argued about what I should give Walter. In the bundle was a white shirt and a pair of white shorts. Both of them were too big for me, and my mother refused to alter them because she said the material was too expensive and too nice to cut up. Instead, we draped the clothes over a chair set up in the living room, and all our neighbors came over to see and feel the silk shirt and linen shorts from Walter VanHarding.

We knew that we could not afford to buy him anything that would be as fine as the clothes he had given me. We also knew that we could not make him the kind of food he was used to. So it was decided that I would give Walter the koa carving that one of my father's friends had carved for me when I was born. The carving was of a carp twisting and fighting against the current, its tail flexed as it thrust its body out of the turbulence, determination and power barely restrained under its scales. It was a carving that had always frightened me as a child; its ferocity was more demon than fish. But my father thought it was an appropriate gift for a sick boy like Walter.

The next Saturday on the bus, I asked my father why he had never mentioned that the VanHardings had a son my age. He said that he had seen Walter only once, when Mrs. VanHarding had my father wash the windows. Walter was lying in bed in a bedroom that faced the back lawn. He said he could see that Walter was very sick but figured that the VanHardings could afford expensive *haole* doctors to take care of him.

"So is that why you decided to accept the gift? Because Walter is sick and might not get well?"

"Yes," he said. "When number one son dying, it is a very sad time. Doesn't matter if they Japanese or not. Everyone sad."

I nodded my head and we remained silent the rest of the way to Mānoa.

My father waited until the afternoon before he sent me to the white house with the gift. The carving was heavy in my arms and was wrapped in the same brown paper and string that Mrs. VanHarding had given us. As I made my way across the back lawn to the kitchen door, I looked into the windows but did not see Walter in any of the rooms. Mrs. VanHarding answered my knock and led me into the kitchen.

"How are you, Mrs. VanHarding," I said from the carefully prepared script that my parents had devised.

"Fine, Masa."

"My parents thank you for the beautiful clothes you have given us." I offered the present to her. "And hope your son will accept this meager gift in return."

"Oh." Mrs. VanHarding looked over her shoulder and then back at me. "You did not have to do that."

"It is nothing so fine as the gift he has given me," I said. Then in proper Japanese fashion, "This gift is worthless and of poor quality." I bowed and held out the present in front of me. "Please accept this token of our gratitude."

According to the script, Mrs. VanHarding was supposed to take the gift, after which I would take a step back, bow again, and then leave. But as I waited, bowed over, she didn't take the gift. I was worried that maybe she wouldn't accept this token of our gratitude because of what I said about it being worthless. These proper Japanese things are always getting me in trouble, I thought.

"Masa?"

I raised my head without straightening up. "You don't want this? It's actually very nice. My mother made me say that part about it being worthless. It's not really…"

"This present is for Walter?"

I nodded.

"Then maybe you should give it to him yourself."

I didn't know what to say. Meeting Walter was not in the script. I was curious about seeing him, maybe through a window, but I wasn't sure I wanted to meet him. I wouldn't know what to say to a sick, rich, *haole* boy. I straightened up and tried to think of a tactful response, when Mrs. VanHarding said, "It would make him happy to meet you."

I knew then I had no choice and said what my father would have wanted me to say: "You honor me."

Mrs. VanHarding motioned for me to follow, and for the first time, I walked out of the kitchen and into the VanHarding world. Even now, it is still hard to describe what I saw there. I can't really describe each room through which we passed. I remember thinking that it took a long time to cross the rooms, and there was something new to look at with every step. At the time, I had never seen so much material used to cover a window, with the excess allowed to spill out onto the walls. I had never seen a wooden floor shine. I had never seen chairs where cloth covered the entire thing, not just the seat. I had never seen doors made of glass. I had never seen plates and bowls and cups and pitchers that reflected like mirrors. I had never seen walls made of books. I had never seen an overhead light made up of diamonds, too numerous to count. But all of that did not prepare me for a sight I had never even seen in my dreams.

"There's a tree in your house," I said to Mrs. Van Harding, but she had already moved to the other side of the room. It must be a mistake, I thought. Why would someone grow a tree in their house?

"Walter, you have a visitor," she said to someone lying on the couch.

I knew that I was supposed to follow Mrs. VanHarding to the other side of the room and give Walter his present. But I did not want to stop looking at the tree. It was a pine tree, of course, but at that time all I knew was that it was a tree shaped like a green mountain, pointy on top and broader on the way down. I was going to touch it and make sure it was real, but I knew my father would not like me touching anything that belonged to the VanHardings.

"Masa," she said, "Masa, we are over here."

I carried the present to where Mrs. VanHarding was calling me but kept my eyes on the tree.

"Walter," she said as I got closer. "This is Masa. The yard boy's son. He is ten, also."

I turned my eyes away from the tree to the boy on the couch. I was surprised to see that Walter, propped up by pillows, was not the tall, fat boy I had envisioned.

Judging by the clothes he had given me, I had expected to see someone who was much taller and much heavier than I was. A boy version of Mrs. VanHarding. Instead, Walter's skin looked as if it didn't quite fit, like he had shriveled inside from staying too long in the ocean. Against his white clothes, his skin took on an ashy hue, like a shirt that had been worn and washed too often. Even his hair looked weary of fighting the advancing white that had taken over his blond roots. When he looked at me, I felt I was looking into the worn-down eyes of an old plantation worker. Eyes that saw everything but kept it on the horizon.

"Hello, Masa."

"Hi…" I didn't know what to say next. I was trying to remember the beginning of the script so I could restart, but the tree and then Walter made me forget. "…Walter."

"Only my parents call me Walter." He smiled at his mother. "Everyone else calls me Walt."

"Yes… Walt," I said and then frantically tried to think of something to say. I watched Mrs. VanHarding squeeze Walter's hand, then walk past the tree out of the room. "The tree," I said to myself, then I noticed Walter looking at me. "You have one in your house… Walt."

"Yes, do you like our Christmas tree?"

"Oh yeah, Christmas." I had heard of Christmas. My parents had used the word once or twice, and one of my friends had said something about Christmas, something he had learned in school, but I always missed school during the last few months of the year. "A Christmas tree."

"This is the biggest tree we've had yet. How big is your Christmas tree?"

Our Christmas tree? I wondered if I should tell him the truth. "Not as big as this one."

"Yes, yes, but how big is it, anyway?"

I was about to reach up with my hands and say, about this big, when I realized I was still carrying the gift and had no way to gesture. "We don't have one."

"Your family doesn't have a Christmas tree?"

"No."

"Why not? What do you do for Christmas? How can you have Christmas without a Christmas tree?" Walter pushed himself a little higher up on the pillows.

Although I didn't know what he was asking, I didn't like the way he was asking it, so I shoved the package at him and said, "Here, here's your gift." I knew it wasn't the proper thing to say, but I didn't care. It was my father's fault for getting me into this in the first place. Why did we always have to give something back? "Here, take it."

"Is this a Christmas present?"

Christmas present? What do I answer? Yes? No? Which answer did he want to hear? I chose yes.

"Well, you have to put it under the tree, then." Walter frowned at me. "Didn't you know that?"

"Yeah," I said and put the gift next to several other boxes that were beneath the tree. It didn't make sense to me, but if he wanted me to put it under the tree…

"Don't you know anything about Christmas?" he asked.

I wanted to say yes because it sounded as if I should know but saying yes got me in trouble last time. "No."

Walter continued frowning while I stood next to the tree. The tree had a pleasant scent, and it reminded me of my sister, Naomi, and the powder we put on her newborn skin.

"You don't know about Santa Claus or Bethlehem?" he asked. I wasn't sure if he was asking me or himself. "Don't you get presents either?"

"Well," I said as I considered his question. "I usually get presents on New Year's Day." Walter swung his legs off the couch and sat up. "And then there's Boy's Day."

"But that's not like Christmas," he said.

"No." I thought about the tree behind me. "I guess not."

We then looked at each other. I could imagine my father kneeling among the orchids, wiping his brow, and wondering what was taking me so long. I was thinking I should probably leave now that my mission had been accomplished, and was just about to make that suggestion when Walter said, "Come here. Sit down."

"Why?" I asked, even though my father had scolded me many times for asking "why" so much. No good ask too many questions, he would say.

"Because I'm going to tell you about Christmas." Walter smiled at me. "I'm going to tell you a Christmas story."

I still don't know why Walter decided to do what he did. I don't think he was trying to convert me to Christianity, because he barely mentioned the baby Jesus and Bethlehem. Or if he did, I didn't remember that part as much as the story about decorating trees and the flying animals and the fat *haole* man with the white beard and how he came through a hole in the ceiling instead of the door and gave you presents, everything you wanted if you were good and had listened to your parents that year. As Walter told the story and I followed his voice and hands, I forgot that he was sick, that he was *haole*, and felt as if I were with any of my Palama friends just talking story. When he finished, he closed his eyes and leaned his head against the back of the couch. Neither of us had anything to say as he breathed heavily and slowly as if asleep. We sat in silence until Mrs. VanHarding appeared in the doorway a few seconds later.

"Masa," she said. I stood up from the couch. "Your father is waiting for you outside."

I nodded at Mrs. VanHarding and turned to say something to Walter. He had opened his eyes and was smiling weakly at me.

"I was just telling Masa a Christmas story," Walter said to his mother as he slid his legs back on the couch. "But we ran out of time before he could tell me a story."

"Well, perhaps next week Masa can tell you a story." She turned to me. "You are coming back next week?"

"Yes," I answered, although she didn't really seem to be asking me. "To tell Walter a story."

"Good," she said and then to Walter, "I will be right back with your medicine after I show Masa out."

Walter nodded. "See you next Saturday, Masa."

"Yes, next Saturday." I nodded. "Walt."

My father did not say a word to me at the VanHardings' kitchen door or the entire bus ride home. Even through dinner, he did not once look at me. So later that night after my mother had cleared the dinner dishes, I was relieved when my father finally said, "Why you cause trouble for the VanHardings?"

"I didn't. Mrs. VanHarding told me to give the gift to Walter. She said that he wanted to meet me, so…"

"You see inside the house?" my mother asked.

"Yes," I said and proceeded to tell them all I could remember. My father did not say anything as I described the things I had seen, but my mother kept interrupting me for more details. What color were the walls, the rugs, the furniture? How big were the rooms, bigger than this house? Was Mrs. Van Harding wearing lots of gold and diamonds? When I got to the part about the tree, my father snorted.

"No make sense, I tell you, "he said. "These *haoles*. Make me cut down live tree and put tree in house. After new year come, make me take tree out of house. Throw tree away."

I knew I had to wait until he was finished. But he didn't say anything else, so I continued. Then, in the middle of my description of Santa and the presents, my father blurted, "And how you throw tree away? Cannot. Got to burn." He lifted his empty teacup. My mother reached over with the teapot and refilled his cup. "Wasting tree, I tell you," he said.

"Go on, Ma-chan," said my mother, and so I did, ending with the part where Walter had finished his story and Mrs. VanHarding was back in the room.

"Mrs. VanHarding," I took a deep breath, "wants me to come back next Saturday."

"Hahh?" Like most Japanese fathers, my father didn't like surprises from his children. "What you mean?"

"It's for Walter. Mrs. VanHarding wants me to help Walter."

"Help? Help with what?"

"She wants me to help him…" For the first time in my life, I lied to my father, "…learn Japanese."

My father started to stand up. "No *shibai*, you!"

"I'm not lying," I lied. "She wants him to learn Japanese."

"Why? Why he like learn Japanese?" He was standing now, looming over me.

"I don't know," I said, scared that this was starting to get away from me like an unraveling ball of yarn rolling downhill. "You told me never to ask why, especially to *haoles*."

"Don't say dumb things!" He raised his arm. My mother started tugging on his shirt but he ignored her. "*Haoles* no like learn Japanese, they like everyone learn English!"

"Let him go, let him go," my mother pleaded. "Maybe she pay extra for teaching."

I nodded at him, knowing that if I opened my mouth again, that hand would come down. He glared at me and I lowered my gaze to my feet. Neither of us spoke and I didn't raise my head until he exhaled loudly and said, "No embarrass us."

I nodded again and started to leave the room. I was almost out when I heard him say, "And no get me fired."

I didn't want to tell my father the truth because I didn't want him and my mother to tell me what story to tell Walter. I knew they would pick a story about one of Japan's glorious samurais who did this or that brave deed and then died violently. Or some story about a child who did not listen to his parents and was tricked by demons and was now enduring eternal punishment. I wanted to tell Walter a story like the one he told me: a story where animals had magical powers and good things happened to children, and at the end of the story everyone was happy.

However, I did not know a story like that. All the stories I had learned from my parents or their friends were not happy enough, and Walter probably knew all the stories I had learned in school. Every day until Saturday, while working with my father at one of the estates or afterward at home, I tried to make up a story. But every story turned out to be a thinly disguised version of the Christmas story, except with a fat Japanese man or flying mongooses. Saturday afternoon found me at the VanHardings' kitchen door, with no story to tell.

"Hello, Masa." Mrs. VanHarding opened the door. "Walter has been waiting for you."

"Is he too tired to see me?" It was my last hope. "I don't have to see him today. Maybe next week?"

"Nonsense," she said. "Come, he's waiting for you in the sitting room." She turned and motioned for me to follow.

I slid my feet after her, barely looking at the things around me. This time, the VanHarding house did not seem so wonderful, just confusing and forbidding. I suddenly understood what my father meant by the *obake* house.

When we entered the sitting room, Walter was on the couch near the Christmas tree. The tree had been decorated with ribbons of red and green, paper cutouts, white candles, garlands of silver, and glass balls that reflected the sunlight. The festivity of the tree only made me feel more empty-handed, like the hollowness I felt when I won a game by cheating. The carving I had given Walter stood unwrapped on a table. Mrs. VanHarding whispered to Walter, turned to smile at me, and left the room.

Walter pointed to the end of the couch. "Hello, Masa. Come sit here."

"Hello, Walt." I was hoping that he forgot I was supposed to tell him a story.

"So, what story are you going to tell me?"

I tried a change of topic. "Your tree looks very nice. Very Christmas."

"My father helped me decorate it," he said. "I did the bottom and he did the top."

Having exhausted all my knowledge on that topic, I switched to another. "Did you like the gift we gave you?"

"Yes, my mother was just telling me that I should remember to thank you for it." We both turned to look at the carving. "So thank you for this very nice... fish."

Both of us started laughing but stopped almost immediately when Walter started to cough. He coughed for a long time, and I waited until he was breathing normally.

"That's why we gave you this fish," I said as I stood up and took the carving off the table. "So you would get better." I handed the carving to Walter. "It's a carp which is good luck for boys."

"Good luck for boys?"

"See this," I pointed to the base of the carving. "This is the water, the current." I pointed to the flank of the fish. "See this? The carp is bursting out of the water. It is a strong fish and can fight off the rough water."

I put Walter's hand along the carved side of the fish. "Can you feel it? It is alive, full of power." He caressed the carving. "The carp is not afraid and does not give up."

And then it came to me. The story I needed to tell.

I drew up my legs onto the couch. "Once there was an old couple who lived in the countryside of Japan. Everything was good, and they lived simple and peaceful lives, farming rice year after year. But there was one thing that was missing. One thing that they really wanted but never had. Something that would make their lives much happier." Out the window, over Walter's shoulder, I could see my father pruning the hedges. I watched him move from one bush to the next, each swing of the sickle fluid and assured, a movement he performed hundreds of times a week. Then somewhere in a dim portion far back in my ten-year-old mind, I thought that if I were lucky, I would be able to move as he did in the world: deliberately and without shame.

"What!" Walter shook my arm. "What was it?"

"A boy," I said. "They wanted a son." I told him the story of Momotarō, the boy born from a peach found by the old couple. I told Walter of how Momotarō grew and brought much happiness to the couple, their lives made brighter by his presence. How Momotarō excelled in school and at games. How he was an expert wrestler and a good swordsman. "Then," I said, "when he was still a young boy, Momotarō decided to kill the demons stealing from his village." I told Walter of Momotarō's journey and of the talking animals he befriended: the dog who could bite through anything, the monkey who was slyer and trickier than any man, the bird who could see further and fly faster than any other animal. I explained how Momotarō was not afraid and sailed to the island where the demons lived and killed them all with the help of his animal friends. How Momotarō returned to the village and gave back everything the demons had stolen. And how, now that the demons were dead, the entire village celebrated but none more than Momotarō's parents who were just happy that their son was home with them.

When I had finally finished, Walter looked up the from the carving he was still holding. "That was a good story."

I nodded. "When you get better, maybe we can play Momotarō sometime." I saw my father brush off his clothes and walk across the lawn toward the house. "Like I do with my friends at home."

"That would be fun," he said. "As long as I get to be Momotarō."

"All right, it's more fun being the monkey anyway." And as soon as I'd said that, Mrs. VanHarding appeared in the doorway.

The next Saturday was the first week of the new year, and I returned to Japanese school. I wish I could say that despite our differences, Walter and I had become steady friends, but in reality I never went back to the VanHarding estate and I never spoke with Walter again. I didn't forget him; my days just became too busy. Regular school during the week, Japanese school afterward and on Saturdays, adventures with my Palama friends on Sunday—it seemed I always had something else to do, something too important to postpone. Then one Saturday halfway into the new year, I came home from Japanese school and found my father already back from work.

"Didn't you go to work today?"

"Yes, but I had to come back."

"Why?" I asked, but I already knew.

"VanHarding boy die two days ago." He shook his head. "Very sad. Funeral today, so no work."

Suddenly, I wanted to tell my father what had really happened between me and Walter and of the story I told. But as the impulse to confess welled up in me, I knew that I wouldn't be able to tell him. I thought of the promise I had made Walter and then abandoned. And as that wave of guilt sucked me out into an ocean of remorse, I turned away from my father, confused.

My father and I never talked about the VanHardings again; I suppose he felt there was no need. I did not understand what it meant that Walter had died and my father could not afford the luxury of dwelling further upon it.

In a few years, my father saved enough money to open up his own restaurant in Palama, the Palama Inn. He gave his old clients to a friend of his, a recent immigrant to the islands. One day this man told my father that the VanHardings had decided to move back to the mainland. Massachusetts, the man said.

Now, years later, after an old man's lifetime of knowing people and then letting them slip out of my life for no reason other than my own laziness, Walter's is the friendship I think about the most. I wonder if I might have become a different person if I had gotten to know Walter better. So in my regret, I do the only thing I am able do. Every year, with my children and now with my grandchildren, I tell them the Christmas story. I tell them also of the boy, Momotarō, and his fearlessness while facing his enemy. And then, when they are ready, I show them the white shirt and shorts and tell them this story.

TRADING HEROES

The only baseball card I ever coveted was of a first baseman for the Atlanta Braves named Mike Lum. This was in 1976, the prime of my baseball card trading years, when I was at the top of my game both in experience and skills. I was a veteran trader from as far back as second grade and had amassed an awesome collection that spanned three decades and almost as many shoeboxes. Although I was consulted a lot on other people's trades—What do you think about being offered a Whitey Ford in his declining years for a '73 Vida Blue and Rollie Fingers?—like an experienced criminal attorney, I was only approached in the most serious trades: someone wanting to trade up for my rookie Mantle or pre-war Williams, for example. I often used my reputation of fear and intimidation to negotiate my exchanges.

At W.O. Gladden Elementary in Kansas City, the only person in the fifth grade who could barter as an equal was my friend, Jimmy, who initiated me into the world of baseball card commerce. He was the middle brother from a family of three boys, and the only one in a family of Sicilian descent whose hair was not dark brown but firecracker red, a trait that had last surfaced from the genetic drift in a nearly forgotten aunt from the old country. I've always thought it was this red hair that accounted for the bravado in his personality that I admired. Outside of my peers, I was a quiet kid, but Jimmy was a ribber among kids, grown-ups, friends, and strangers. He could not let a situation pass without comment, and he often ventured into the good, bad, and inappropriate for a laugh. He was fearless about making fun of everyone to their faces, even his parents, an action that in my family would have been akin to condemning myself to death.

He was one of my oldest friends more by happenstance than by devotion, since both our fathers were officers in the Air Force and worked in the same unit. As a result, our families were sometimes stationed together at the same base, moving in tandem at the will of the Air Force. He joked that I had to remain his friend because my dad worked for his dad, and "You gotta suck up to the boss's son." But in reality, he was the only friend I had known longer than two years, the typical duration of my father's postings.

Perhaps because Jimmy was my baseball card mentor, he was also my fiercest opponent. He had a completely dispassionate attitude about baseball cards. In his hands, the cards were mere commodities, the players just value indicators like the designs on a bill, for the part that really interested him: the transaction. He was a consummate capitalist with a robber-baron mentality that even grown-ups could recognize. Once, sitting in the back of my family's station wagon, we were trying to complete our fifth-grade homework. We were discussing a problem that had stumped us for miles, one quarter plus one quarter plus one tenth, when from the driver's seat my dad asked, "If I gave you two quarters and one dime, how much money would you have?"

"Sixty cents," Jimmy said instantly.

My dad, raised in a generation that taught that sons could learn all they needed by silence rather than explication, paused to let this lesson sink in.

"Six tenths," I said finally in amazement at my dad's creativity, "that's our answer, Jimmy, six tenths."

But I could tell Jimmy didn't get it. He was still looking at my dad, thinking about the sixty cents that might be coming to him.

If I had one liability as a trader, it was a touch of sentimentality, a penchant that drove me at times to make irrational trades—like a '54 Bob Feller for a Vince DiMaggio—just so I could complete the DiMaggio brothers trio: Vince, Dom, and Joe. Jimmy knew this about me and exploited my weakness to the fullest. Rather than deal with specific trades of such-and-such player for his Mike Lum, he instead dealt in options: Since it was obvious that he was the only one I knew who owned—what was his name again? Ah yes, card #208 Mike Lum—he would be willing to trade said card #208, for two… no, better make it three cards of his choosing from my entire collection. Such was the brutality of his methods.

I never told Jimmy directly that I wanted the card, but with the instincts of a used car salesman, he had surmised my desire from the feigned disinterest I tried to show the card every time I thumbed through his collection. If I didn't pause to look at it, he would wait until I was well past the card before he fished it out of the stack again, parading it in front of me, wondering aloud why I wanted that card so much. And who wouldn't wonder? As a baseball card, it was nothing special, it wasn't an action shot from an actual game like the '76 Johnny Bench, just up from his crouch, mask off, rising from the dust after making a play at the plate. The Mike Lum card was a staged figure card in the most generic of poses: standing in the field, not even at the plate, the bat resting on his shoulder, with an indifferent grin aimed at the camera. It exuded none of the fierce competitiveness I associated with professional baseball. Even in Lum's best year of 1973, when he batted .294, with eighty-two RBIs and sixteen home runs, that card in mint condition commands only a humble fifty cents. Not exactly an investment-grade instrument.

As a player, Mike Lum wasn't any great shakes, either. He wasn't The Hammer. He never held a batting title in the league or even on the team. Mike Lum was solid and dependable, a journeyman player who had come up through the ranks to earn his starting spot on the roster. He had none of the flashy pizzazz of a Mays or even the sex appeal of a young George Brett. Mike Lum was the kind of guy you hired to plug a hole in your defense, not the kind of guy you created your game plan around.

Aspiring to the Major Leagues myself, I practiced my fielding in the backyard regularly, throwing the baseball as hard as I could against the concrete foundation of the house, then running down the grounders that came barreling back at me. I was the starting shortstop for my team, a position for which I was always picked even though I did not have the feline quickness required for the spot. Even at that age, I knew I wouldn't be able to improve my reflexes, so I worked at the only things I knew I could improve: my fielding and my stupidity. What I couldn't stop with my practiced glove, I would stop with my body, and this willingness to step into the path of the ball was considered a rare ability in the jittery Little League.

On Sundays, my father also joined me in the backyard, ostensibly to do yard work, but little by little drawing closer to me and offering me advice in his usual father-as-coach manner: "Are you an old lady? Bend your back and get that glove all the way down to the ground… What kind of move was that? This is baseball, not ballet—don't anticipate, just move toward the ball… Jesus H. Christ! The job of an infielder is to stop the ball before it gets past you, not to watch the ball go by and then try and stop it!" This continued as it always did until he was throwing me the grounders himself, spicing up the fare with an occasional line drive ("You just dropped the easiest out in baseball!") or pop fly ("You should be thinking of the infield fly rule right now. Explain it to me!"), leaving the lawn mower idling in the corner of the yard, snuffling like an abandoned child.

Eventually his keen eye picked up on my throwing motion, a gruesome sight that caused him, I believe, real physical pain not unlike an ulcer. Although he had been the person who taught me how to throw a baseball, I threw, in his words, "worse than a girl, like a duck almost." The textbook throwing method he had tried to instill in me—three-quarters over the top, upper arm parallel to the ground, hand pointing at ten o'clock, and cranking the whole assembly forward—never felt natural, so I had developed a kind of throwing shorthand: not throwing the ball so much as propelling it with an ungainly push. A push, I might add, that had speed and accuracy and could, from shortstop or third base, nail a runner down going to first. Nevertheless, every time my father noticed it, he would speculate on the physics of my motion and wonder aloud how I managed to get the ball moving at all.

Eventually he would try and reteach me how to throw, winding his arm back and snapping it forward in an exaggerated, heuristic motion that sent the ball rocketing to me, where it slammed into my glove with a bone-splitting crack. This day, perhaps because I was tired out by the fielding practice earlier, I did not even attempt to follow his example, and he became increasingly agitated. His throws came harder and harder at me, and I threw the ball back more and more limply, hoping that by association he would also start throwing weakly. I allowed my concentration to stray just a bit, indulging in nostalgic remembrance of my carefree practices with the wall, when an explosion jarred me from my reveries. When I came to, I was flat on my back with the taste of blood in my mouth, staring up into the blue summer sky. My mother hovered over me, berating my father for his carelessness.

We all moved inside, where my father went into the kitchen to suffer more abuse from my mother and get his usual post–yard work beer. I retreated to the family room where I could tend to my wounds in front of the television.

A few minutes later, my dad came in and watched me nurse my bloody nose. "Use your glove next time," he said as he handed me a box of tissues, "That's what it's for."

"Okay," I said, accepting the tissues and the apology.

That being done, he directed me to turn the channel. I dialed through Gilligan's Island and the PGA until I got to something we both could watch, a live game between the Braves and the Reds.

"The Reds will win," I said, having unquestioningly swallowed the marketing of The Big Red Machine.

"We can watch anyway, can't we," snapped Dad.

I shrugged and purposefully made elaborate ministrations to my nose.

My father preferred an equitable, nonverbal approach to watching ball games on television, grunting up in appreciation when either team made a good play or hit, and grunting down in chastisement when someone performed poorly. Watching in this manner turned a baseball game from a competition between good and evil into a study of the game itself, and as such, a burden to those of us who liked to cheer undeservedly for our team and boo mercilessly at the enemy. At the time, the only benefit I could see from watching games his way was the calm *c'est la vie* attitude he exuded at the end of the game, having sided with neither the victor nor the victim in the contest.

So I knew something unusual was happening when in the midst of the third inning, my dad said, "Ahh, there he is."

"Who?" I asked, scanning the screen.

"There, the first baseman," my father said, pointing to the screen. "Mike Lum."

"Who's Mike Lum?"

My dad was struck mute by my ignorance. The look on his face at that moment must have mirrored the one he had earlier when he realized that I had done nothing to prevent a baseball from hitting me in the face.

"He's our favorite player," he finally answered.

"He is?" My dad had never mentioned having a favorite player before, preferring to praise individual performances or special talents, like Aaron's run for the record or Seaver's concentration on the mound.

"Of course," he said. "He's the first major leaguer from home."

Home was Hawaii, the place where all my relatives and grandparents lived, the place where both my parents were born and raised, and the only mooring post, in our nomadic military life, that we ever meant when we talked about "going home."

Suddenly, I felt I knew Mike Ken-Wai Lum personally, as if he had been a friend of the family for years. I could envision the scene at his parents' house right now, aunties and uncles and cousins who, well, looked like my aunties and uncles and cousins sitting down to watch the game of their boy who had "made it." From the dining table, I could smell the food I missed so much, sushi, poi, kalua pig. I could even see his old baseball coach from Roosevelt High School in Honolulu, sitting back on the sofa watching the game, telling his wife for the thousandth time, "See, I told you. I always knew that boy would make it." At that moment, the entire gallery of my baseball heroes: Gehrig for guts, Mantle for bat, Robinson for fielding, dropped away in an instant for this Atlanta Brave whom, I was sure, had still retained the lilting rhythms and peculiar slang of the Hawaiian Pidgin English that I loved to listen to every time we phoned home to Grandma.

"At first base, huh?"

"Umm," he said. But instead of settling back into his silence, he leaned slightly forward as if to see the television better. "I wanted to go professional once."

I froze. This kind of talk during a game was unprecedented and I didn't know what to expect next. I remained quiet for fear of breaking the spell.

"And I think I would have made a pretty good first baseman."

I didn't doubt it. I had watched him play for the Air Force teams and had seen the intensity he brought to the games. He was solid, focused, and consistent, always waiting for the umpire to call a runner out before rising from his stretch. Even his teammates recognized his reliability and had taken to calling him Mr. Responsibility. Ask any major league manager, they'll tell you that someone named Mr. Responsibility is the person they would want to guard their right corner.

"First base is the kind of position everyone thinks they can play," he said staring at the screen, "but it's a thinking man's position. Your head always has to be in the game. A first baseman is involved with probably 90 percent of the plays in the game. Few can play it well."

I nodded my head in agreement. I had never thought of first base in that way, having always reserved the position as the last stop for the overweight and over-the-hill players whose bats were too big to retire.

"I could have gone semi-pro. I had some offers. But I had just finished college and the war was on and I didn't want to get drafted into the infantry, so I went and volunteered with the Air Force. By the time that was over, why, I had already married and you were coming along and the Air Force seemed like a pretty good place to have a career, and well…" His voice trailed off. In the wake of silence that followed, I could think of nothing to say that would console him.

"God," he said, "I loved the game so much, I used to sleep with that mitt."

My younger sister entered the room at that point and Dad and I said nothing more the rest of the afternoon. But for the rest of that game, I spent as much time watching him as I did the television.

More changed for me that day than my newborn desire to own a Mike Lum baseball card. By the next season, I had begun to spurn the vainglorious position of shortstop as all quickness and light and become enamored with first base. My father and I abandoned our peppery fielding drills for close exercises in subtlety and concentration, so that I could become, in his words, "a perfect first baseman, a player of composure." He trained me in the arcane lore of the position: how to plant my foot on the corner of the bag so a runner could not dislodge it, how to open myself up as a target for the infielders, how to stretch that extra little bit to shave down the lead of a quick runner. At the end of my first season as the team's starting first baseman, they awarded me a new nickname, Jr. Responsibility, and Dad awarded me a new first baseman's mitt. An ugly contraption, it looked like the bastard offspring of an illicit union between a worn-out catcher's mitt and a desperate oven mitt. But like a good first baseman, it was completely utilitarian.

The day I turned "one day short," a military term for one's last day on base, I took my final trip to Jimmy's house. The next morning we would be flying out to my dad's new assignment at Yongsan Post in Seoul, Korea, and Jimmy's dad would be transferring to Mississippi a few weeks later. I was armed with a shoebox of my top-shelf cards, the premium material: my Lou Gehrig card, my Sandy Koufax card, my Willie Mays (true, in his twilight years in a Mets uniform) and my entire set of both the championship '72 Oakland A's and Cincinnati Reds cards, whole team sets that I had laboriously collected. I was even prepared to break one of our unwritten rules: I had brought my Bart Starr and Gale Sayers football cards, willing to trade cross-sport and risk introducing, at the very last minute, a whole new calculus. We sat down on his younger brother's bed, the bottom mattress on a set of bunks, which Jimmy commandeered as his office during the day, and I prepared to deal. I dove into Jimmy's pile of baseball cards and with no pretense, for there was no time, pulled out card #208. No words were spoken; we both knew what I wanted. I opened my shoebox and waited for him to make the first move. I was a warrior primed my whole life for this battle and I was prepared to throw myself upon my sword and fight down to my last card if I had to.

He picked up the Mike Lum card and studied it slowly, once again, from front to back. This was something he did only with this card, preferring to discern the value of the cards from the fear of his opponent. He always inspected the Mike Lum card with the same quizzical look on his face; perhaps he had missed something, something he would be able to read from the stats on the back of the card at the last minute. Finally he shook his head, sighed, and put the card into his shirt pocket. "Let's go outside," he said.

The day was very cold, winter tapering off to a wicked tail that blew knives through us and froze the hard-packed snow onto the earth. We crossed his backyard and climbed to the top of the hill behind his house, neighborhood common property that we nevertheless considered ours. Over the winter we had terraced the hill with mounds of snow and spent our weekends carving out a sledding course with teeth-rattling, gut-impaling moguls along one side and, along the other side, a death-defying speed course that twisted sinuously through a stand of trees. However, our proudest construction, and the one that we reserved for ourselves, was a monstrous ramp that lay in the middle of the steepest part of the hill, which we had watered until it was as slick as a ski jump. One of us would add a new feature to the ramp, a left-hand twist to the exit or a greater curl to the end so that our launches would land us on our backs, and then dare the other to try it. The ramp had grown into an amalgamation of perverse stunts, a record of our sadistic imaginations over the long winter. We stood at the top of the hill for a long time, neither of us saying anything, he with Mike Lum safely ensconced within his jacket, and I with my shoebox under my arm, surveying our creation.

Although it was not yet dinnertime, the evening had surrendered quickly to night and the darkness was pouring like ink over the land. Soon we would hardly be able to see. Finally, Jimmy turned to me and said, "Do you think we'll still be best friends next year?"

I was stunned by the question. Neither of us had ever mentioned anything about being best friends. We never felt the need for confessions of that sort. Yet, as soon as he said it, I knew he was correct. It dawned on me that this must be the way of true best friends, neither needing to speak about it. "I don't know," I answered.

He didn't say anything, and we both knew my answer had been inadequate. We could see our mothers through the windows in his house, getting the dishes ready for the last big feast between our two families. Both our mothers had prepared their specialties: Jimmy's mom had made her Italian sausage and apple pies, and my mom had made her wontons and sweet-and-sour spareribs. "Probably not," I decided.

Jimmy just nodded, and I felt a sudden relief as it became clear to me that he had been thinking the same thing. We watched as Jimmy's mother walked out the back door looking for us, soon joined by my mother, both of them retreating back inside when they could not find us in the darkness at the top of the hill. Jimmy fished around in his jacket and then flipped me Mike Lum. "Here," he said, "you can have this."

I looked at Jimmy. I looked at the card in my hand. I repeated these movements one more time before I could think of something to say. "I can trade you for it," I said, motioning to the box.

"Nah," he said, "let's go." He started walking down the hill toward his house, but I was still too dazed to move.

"What do you want for it?" I called after him. He didn't say anything. I wanted to trade him for it. I had been prepared for a long, grueling night of negotiations, angry words, betrayals, and last-minute desperation tactics. Haggling had always been part of our relationship. I ran up alongside him. "How about this? Or these?"

I even pulled out my Babe Ruth Batting Champion card, not a real Babe Ruth player card, but the only baseball card we had ever seen that had the Babe's picture on it. I had traded with someone's father to get it and we both considered the card one of my better deals. Jimmy didn't even look at me and continued his silent walk toward the house.

We were almost to the back door and I was getting desperate. "Here, take this," I said and handed him the whole box.

But Jimmy just ignored me and walked through the back door, where I followed. We located our spots at the kids' table and sat down for our families' final meal together.

We moved the next day, and a couple of months later in Korea, I gave away my entire sports card collection to my sister, who was just then entering the prime of her trading card years. I had lost interest since I couldn't find a sparring partner as good as Jimmy. His sleight of hand and cold calculations had always kept me teetering at the razor's edge of trading exhilaration or failure. I kept the really good cards for myself—the Hall of Famers and of course, Mike Lum. But my sister never approached the cards as I did. Her temperament was more like that of a private collector: organizing the cards first by year and then by team, instead of by value as Jimmy and I had preferred, noting which ones she was missing and trying to find those by buying packs of cards. She never really traded because she couldn't bear to part with something that she owned.

I saw Jimmy again, when I moved to St. Louis for graduate school and he lived a few hours away in rural Illinois. He is now a mortgage broker with his own 800 number. He still trades as a hobby, but instead of cards, he now trades cars. His most recent trade involved exchanging his early-eighties dandelion-yellow Corvette for a worn-around-the-edges, sixties-model steel-blue convertible Mercedes, a much less common car and hence a greater value. He traded the car with a professor at the university I attended. "Someone you might know," he told me, as if we all belonged to the same secret club. He seemed to delight in the fact that he had gotten the upper hand over this economics scholar.

Once, I even cautiously brought up our final baseball card trade, at the wedding of Jimmy's younger (no longer littler) brother. Jimmy, though, seemed to have forgotten all about Mike Lum, talking instead about other cards he had taken at a steal, and what those cards are now worth and how those people must be kicking themselves. Neither of us has ever mentioned our conversation at the top of the hill on that cold winter evening, but with best friends, sometimes you don't need to.

LOST BOYS

They swarmed our lane like invaders from another planet, hastily parking their vehicles with the lights still on, disgorging fully formed in their light blue containment suits and face shields. Like medieval warriors clutching specialized arms to prod, poke, and grab, they joined their fellow hazmat brethren already engaged in the labeling, photographing, and depositing of dead chickens in industrial black drums. We on Muliwai Lane had never considered ourselves in danger; in fact, finding dead chickens in the gutters of our lane was an occasional occurrence when Chicken Charlie was on a bender. It took a couple of days before someone finally called the authorities, and only because the carcasses that were piling up under our hedgerows and hibiscus were inviting legions of horseflies whose incessant humming was starting to keep us from our sleep.

The spacemen roamed our neighborhood most of the afternoon, hoisting bags of suspect chicken feed into the beds of trucks, disinfecting the areas where fluids had stained, and poisoning the soil to keep the maggots from rooting. They noted the location of each dead chicken by spraying a yellow X where each one was found till it looked like a curse written in an arcane script had been painted in ocher at the edges of our lane. It was late in the day before they entered the house and followed the tracks of bloody footprints into a corner of the kitchen to find Chicken Charlie nearly naked in a pool of blood, cowering in the corner with his butchering blade in his hand. But it was us kids who dared approach the police as they led away a covered-up but still bloodstained Chicken Charlie, to ask, "What happened to Chick? Where is Chicken Charlie's son?"

Long before a certain colonel from Kentucky pimpled the islands with his gleaming red-and-white plastic huts, the most famous chicken man on Oahu was Chicken Charlie. Chicken Charlie started each day by loading his pushcart with a flock of live chickens and pushing them down to the docks of Honolulu. He would butcher the chickens there on the dock and trade the entrails with the fishermen who used them for chum in the lucrative sport fishing charters. In exchange, Chicken Charlie would get enough ice to pack his chicken parts for the day, before he moved off a short ways to the other side of the docks where he would find the longshoreman captain. Bribed by the promise of free fried chicken, the captain would direct a couple of his men to rip open some wooden crates and stack the waste wood onto the end of the pushcart. Chicken Charlie quickly built a fire in the fifty-five-gallon drum that he kept on his cart and stoked it with longshoreman wood until it was hot enough to curdle a cauldron of yesterday's cooking oil, which he skimmed with a wooden paddle until it was as clear as rainwater. After the promised pieces were cooked, wrapped in newspaper, and sent to the longshoreman captain, Chicken Charlie would make his first sales of the day there on the dock, feeding the hungry longshoremen just coming off the night shift, and catching the arrival of the day shift workers who, despite having just eaten breakfast, could not help but succumb to the smell of the fried chicken and indulge themselves with a few pieces.

By mid morning he had exhausted the pocket change of the longshoremen and would move off to the more fertile hunting grounds of downtown Honolulu. There he parked his pushcart across the street from the Bank of Hawaii building, stoked up his fire some more, and prepared for the lunch crowd. His regulars came early for the dark-meat legs and thighs, and if he was lucky enough to catch a good trade wind, Chicken Charlie might lure customers and tourists from as far away as Iolani Palace to sell out everything by early afternoon. If not, he would wheel his pushcart from the corner of Pauahi and King, leaving behind the smell of smoke and fried chicken and a puddle of water tinged with blood, and make his way back to the docks for the arrival of the most highly paid longshoremen, the swing shift.

Year after year of this unalterable route, six days a week, led to a small fortune that Chicken Charlie periodically drained through his bouts with alcohol. We kids on the lane learned to stay away from him then, to not beg him for the crispy leavings of fried breading and chicken skin that he usually saved for us and we shared with each other like popcorn. He was a violent and unpredictable drunk, often banging on our house doors and demanding redress from our parents for an imagined slight that may have happened years ago, or swinging wildly at one of us if we came too near, as he spewed curses and spit, mistaking us for an apparition he was already battling in his foggy imagination. His chickens would go unattended then, settling themselves in the low trees and banks of Nu'uanu Stream, and inevitably falling victim to some of the feral cats that prowled there. We also knew when Chicken Charlie was out of money and back from the bottle because the chickens were in their coops and small newspaper-wrapped peace offerings of fried chicken could be found on our porches in the morning.

All might have remained this way, were it not for the Great Dock Strike. With the longshoremen out of work and being fed through the strike funds of the union, Chicken Charlie lost not only a major market, but also his wood supplier. This forced him to wake up even earlier and trade quickly with the fishermen so that he could scour construction sites in Honolulu for waste wood before the first construction workers arrived at full light. And that was how he got caught by the church ladies.

Chicken Charlie had been raiding the wood pile for the annex extension of Kawaiaha'o Church for some time, finding it convenient to load up on wood there before pushing his cart the short five blocks to his downtown post. It had become such a regular part of his routine since the strike that one early morning he failed to notice the flickering lights inside the church that had dimly illuminated the stained glass windows. When the annex door burst open releasing the Ladies Auxiliary from a special sunrise service, they caught Chicken Charlie in mid hoist, brilliantly aglow in the light from the candles the ladies were holding.

Both sinner and saints silently gaped at each other. Then an impulse to run seized Chicken Charlie and he dropped the board he was carrying but took less than a step before he realized that he could not abandon his pushcart. He looked down at his feet instead, and the ladies looked at each other and nodded silently, for nothing motivates a group of charity-hearted women more than a cause, and clearly, standing in front of them just outside their church door was the most pathetic cause of all: a man who needed saving.

They clustered around Chicken Charlie in their muumuus and candles and started speaking to him all at once. For the first time in his life, Chicken Charlie knew fear. Unaccustomed to the company of women or even to speaking in sentences at all—his daily conversations having become scripted grunts and gestures with old salt fishermen and leatherneck longshoremen—Chicken Charlie felt the peppering of their questions like physical blows to his body. He staggered backwards to the pushcart for support and managed to discern that they were not angry so much as curious about why he needed the wood. The women grew silent as they watched him leap onto his pushcart, layer wood into his fifty-five-gallon drum, take one of their candles, and nurture a fire from an orange candle flame to a roaring white cooking fire.

He served them fried chicken that morning while they inquired about his technique, his marinade recipe, his timing for cooking the different pieces so that they came out light and crispy and not laden with grease. They cooed over his industry and economy, and later, paid him for all the chicken he had served. But by then, Chicken Charlie couldn't have cared less. He had been drawn in by their charms, their fluttering hand gestures, even their smell, and would have agreed to anything to spend some more time with them. And so he did. In exchange for picking up a small amount of daily waste wood, Chicken Charlie would have to attend Sunday morning church services every week, under the auspices of the Ladies Auxiliary.

For almost a year, Chicken Charlie was a regular fixture of that congregation, the proud trophy of the Ladies Auxiliary. Shined up and newly sober, he started implementing some welcome changes on our lane as well. Chicken Charlie cleaned up his property, secured his pens, cut back the brush all the way to Nu'uanu Stream, and even repainted his house and storage sheds. He was like a hen sprucing up her nest for a new arrival, and sure enough, not long after the paint had dried on the house, Chicken Charlie picked up a catalog called "Ladies of Luzon" and ordered himself a new bride from the Philippines.

It's hard to remember now exactly what she looked like. In Chick's face, the way he held his body, there was no trace of his mother, as if he had inherited all of his physical characteristics from one parent. And maybe that's what she saw when she gave birth and glimpsed the misbegotten head of her newborn son and the old-man features staring back at her. Maybe she took it as an omen, a vision of the future and the lifetime of toil that awaited her, so she fled the hospital, not even waiting to nurse her son for the first time, and disappeared.

Having been abandoned by his wife and betrayed by God, something inside Chicken Charlie became hard, turned over, and died. He stopped attending church, took up his pushcart seven days a week instead of taking a day off, and returned to the docks. He made only two changes to his pushcart: he created a makeshift sling padded generously at the head to tote his newborn son, and he built a rectangular cubbyhole on the underside of his cart just big enough to store a large bottle of whiskey.

Forced to take his son with him everywhere, he grew fiercely loyal to the boy and intolerant of anyone who looked at the child too long or said a word about him. He had come to believe that he and his son were not bound by the rules that governed other men, and kept the boy to himself, away from public education, to teach him the bitter lessons that Chicken Charlie had learned in life. The two were inseparable, and so the boy was christened Chick.

Some of us say the fighting chickens came next and some say the beatings, but we all agree that by age six, Chick had become something like a wild animal: untamable, unruly, and uncommunicative. Baby Chick, the precious white grub cocooned in the sling from the handles of his father's pushcart, had been borne by Chicken Charlie with defiance and pride, like an old war wound. But even the most powerful symbols change over time, and Chick became not only a financial burden to Chicken Charlie but the manifestation of his failures that rose and confronted him every morning and waited to greet him at the end of every long day. So Chicken Charlie turned to the only solution he knew: he struck out at his failures in alcohol-fueled rages that sometimes lasted all night, as if beating his melon-headed son were an offering to a wretched and unfeeling god who had chosen Chicken Charlie as his vessel of misery.

Mornings found Chick among his only friends, the chickens and roosters he raised for slaughter. While the rest of the kids on the lane went to school, Chick was locked inside the chicken pen of his yard, wandering from coop to coop, tending to his charges. We dragged him to school once, helping him dig a shallow pit that would allow his massive head and shoulders to pass under the fence. All of us arrived dirty and late for school, but once the teachers saw Chick's dented cranium and bulging forehead, they forgot their objections and excused our tardiness. That day, for perhaps the first time in his life, Chick was treated like just a regular kid. All morning he doodled with pencil and paper, treating each trip to the pencil sharpener with profound amazement at the simple crank that could produce such miracles. He stopped only when the teacher read to us from our Hawaiian history and legends text; nodding as if the wars, betrayals, and human sacrifices were just another type of chicken fight except more distant since he had had no hand in raising the combatants.

Because he didn't know better, Chick ate everything from his tray for lunch, including the bean casserole, cobbled together from leftovers from two days of green beans served earlier in the week. Then he amazed us again by consuming a second helping on a large faculty tray that the lunch ladies, charmed by his voracious appetite, brought to him.

That afternoon, he spent the day in the corner of the classroom with the school counselor, who tested him with a variety of flash cards and pictures and learned what we kids could have told her if she had just asked one of us—that

Chick could understand almost everything that was said to him, but he could neither read nor write. Chick walked back home with us from school clutching a letter the counselor had written to Chicken Charlie, and we helped him crawl back under the chicken fence, promising to get him again tomorrow morning.

That was the last of Chick we would see for awhile.

It must have been the school who called the authorities and sent them out to Chicken Charlie's house. He claimed to have sent Chick away, "to distant relatives on the mainland," he told them, "at a special school." Having not seen Chick for a couple of weeks we actually believed him, hoping that maybe now Chick was in a better place, sitting at a desk with pencil in hand, doodling under the watchful eye of a kindhearted teacher while we slept in our beds, several time zones away.

But when Chicken Charlie stopped working for a couple of days to build an enormous privacy fence around his property, boards mated so snugly that not even a shadow could slide between them, we knew that the brief cries and strangulated sobs we sometimes heard at night were not a hen being taken by a feral cat, but the voicing of Chick still under the savage hand of his father.

We kids on the lane debated among ourselves whether we should tell the teachers or not, for the last time had caused an outburst so severe that Chick now seemed to walk with a limp (at least that's what it sounded like from the other side of the fence when we called his name and he paused before resuming his shuf-fle-drag-shuffle). In the end, though, we did tell one teacher, the youngest teacher we had, the one who had read to him most of the morning. She looked at us in alarm, then looked away to her desk at the front of the classroom and slowly start-ed nodding. She walked over and took the Hawaiian History and Legends text from her desk and handed it to us.

"Make sure he gets this," she told us, as she handed us her teacher's edition with all the extra pictures and stories. "You will have to read it to him."

And so we did. Every day after school, one of us would sit by the fence and knock until we heard Chick's hurried shuffling on the other side, and in a few moments the book would appear from under the fence wrapped carefully in news-paper as if it were some holy relic instead of the ballast that weighted down every kid's bookbag on the lane. It seemed to matter little where we started or what we read to him, he seemed as pleased to hear about the legends of the man-eating shark gods as he was to hear about the arcane details of Sanford Dole's appoint-ment as president of the Provisional Government during the overthrow of Queen Liliuokalani, as long as we ended our readings with his favorite story, the legend of the boy warriors of Kipapa Gulch.

It was a legend that did not appear in our regular kid texts but was found only in the teacher's edition. The illustration that accompanied the story showed a group of five to six shaggy-headed boys of varying ages, all of them nearly naked except for brief *malo* loincloths, leaning on long sticks, standing on a cap rock overlooking Kipapa Gulch. With their skin indelibly dyed rust red from the iron-rich soils of central Oahu, they stood out like bloody centurions against the regal blue sky of the background. According to legend, these boys were castoffs from ancient Hawaiian society: young criminals or *kapu* breakers, parricides, or the sons of disgraced men. These runaways would escape the judgment of their communities by escaping to Kipapa Gulch, where they shed all trappings of their former lives, including their names, and adopted the reclusive culture and strange, guttural tongue of the boy warriors. Ferocious and ritualistically brutal in the way of young savages, these boys were highly feared and often the targets of unsuccessful suppression programs by the kings of ancient Oahu. It was Kamehameha who recognized the political value of these boy warriors and struck a deal with them: If the boys would side with him on his great assault on Oahu and its king, Kalanikūpule, they would be granted Kipapa Gulch for self-rule in perpetuity. And when King Kamehameha became sovereign over all the islands, he issued that royal edict, the text stated, one that has never been revoked.

Technically, the legend ended there. But every time we pushed the text under the fence, it would come right back to us, open to the story of the boy warriors. Figuring that Chick couldn't read anyway, we turned the page and pretended there was more. We told him about how boys came out only at night and so they were never seen, but you could tell how far away they were from their howling on the wind. It was only the following morning, when you found a blood-red footprint on your porch or smelled the pungent iron-in-the-rain scent they left behind, did you realize that they had deceived you and had been close enough to slit your throat while you slept. Killers by profession and not for sport, they ate mostly pineapple and sugarcane stolen from the fields. They drank water from irrigation ditches. Workers who found the leavings from one of their feasts—discarded pineapple tops, smoldering campfires surrounded by the circular ripples of footprints of some primal dance—never reported the sightings for fear of retribution, preferring instead to incur the wrath of the planters and overseers for the thin harvest.

We saved the best part for last because even we fervently believed that it could be so: to never have to brush their teeth because the boys slept on the ground, and during the night the ants would clean their teeth while they were sleeping. To never have to bathe because their skin was permanently stained the same rust color as the dirt, leaving only the whites of their eyes as evidence of their former existence. These descriptions brought sighs from both sides of the fence, and that was how we knew we were done and could pass the book back to Chick.

The next five years brought more of the same routine, except while we grew up tall and slender and straight, nurtured in equal measure by the sun and the challenges and expectations of school, Chick seemed to grow both more bulky and more wilted. A callus of muscle built up along his shoulders and upper back to protect him from the sun beating down on him during the day and his father at night. This, in addition to his oversized head, had unbalanced him and he lumbered around hunched over as if in constant supplication, like Atlas bending under the weight of the world.

We had higher hopes for him once. For a little while, it looked like Chicken Charlie was training Chick to become his assistant. We would see them wheeling around Honolulu on their rounds, Chick pushing the cart while Chicken Charlie talked to him constantly, like an attentive vocational trainer. Afterward, Chick proudly raised his hands over the fence to show us the blisters that were forming on his palms, but in less than week, Chick was locked back into his pen during the days, while his father worked the fried-chicken trade alone. It seemed that the downtown chicken business fell off precipitously when Chick assisted, and Chicken Charlie blamed Chick's brutish appearance for spoiling the appetites of the city gentry. In truth, it was Chicken Charlie's hostility that turned away his customers. Whenever they made a sympathetic comment or inquired about his son's condition, Chicken Charlie would berate them with threats and insults until they withdrew, cash still in hand. Then later at home, Chicken Charlie would curse himself and then his son for his own foolish notions.

With the door of the world finally closed to him, Chick turned his attention to the only thing left to him, his brood. We would learn later that Chicken Charlie was earning a growing reputation for himself as a breeder and trainer of a peculiar line of fighting cocks. These cocks were not the overly aggressive and simple-minded type that dominated the sport; rather, Chicken Charlie produced a stable of cocks that were dopey and punchy, much like his own son. Some possessed peculiar neurological tics, and some claimed that the chickens' slow reaction times proved that they were retarded, but nevertheless, once the blood started flying, these chickens were extremely deadly.

Chick started off as something of a mascot to these combatants, an inside joke on defective genetics, just another cruel amusement to the whole spectacle.

But once Chicken Charlie started proving the success of his line and the pile of dead chickens grew as fast as his financial backers, Chick threw himself into the process and became something of a chicken master. No one would have suspected that it was Chick who selected the crosses for breeding, who handled all the nurturing, exercise, and feeding for the gamecocks, who toughened them up for their much-speculated masochistic fighting technique, and who sewed the victors back up after matches.

Some would say later that Chick did this to avoid being beaten, that the late-night raging and scuffling did not crescendo on the nights Chicken Charlie won, but we kids knew better. We knew it was more than that to Chick. He had stopped wanting us to read to him, stopped coming by the fence at the appointed time. We knew he had discovered a new religion, with a new text, written in the blood of a dusty fighting ring. His fighting cocks, winners for a short time but all losers eventually, were mere sacrifices of love to that greater god, his father. And we kids, laboring under the disappointment and expectations of our own fathers, recognized that and even started thinking as Chick did: That this was all right. That we were okay. That I am okay.

And then Chicken Charlie found a doctor for the operation.

To save your life, he told his son.

It had been over a decade since a reputable doctor had suggested that Chick undergo corrective procedures for his cranial and neurological deformities. These operations, once possible as an infant, were now deemed too risky to the crucial connections and pathways that had developed in Chick's brain. At the very least, Chick's personality would change, but the doctors listed other consequences: degradation of motor skills, hearing or vision loss, and the menacing "cascading of the autonomic nervous system," which, "while impossible to predict," seemed less uncertain in outcome: death or a permanent vegetative state.

Who could know, really, what lay in the heart of Chicken Charlie when he conspired with a cabal of unlicensed doctors in Chinatown to summon the same from Hong Kong to perform this surgery. Some will say it was a selfish act to free himself, to loose the anchor of his past and escape the responsibility of his mistakes. Yet we on the lane want to believe that he acted out of some deeper and more primal motivation, perhaps a kind of love darkened with the chiaroscuro of guilt. The kind of love all fathers have for their sons, a protective talisman handed down from generations to mend the mistakes of their own past and give their sons a better future.

Then came days of dead chickens and investigations.

They would find traces of Chick, some of his blood in the kitchen, some possible footprints among many at the scene, even his clothes strewn up the banks of Nu'uanu Stream with bloody and muddied handprints all over them, as if he had been running and his clothes had been ripped off his body in anger. But they never actually found him, and Chicken Charlie's silence, the evidence, and the bloodied deboning knife were enough for the prosecutors to charge Chicken Charlie with murder.

The trial would expose the secret of Chicken Charlie's success in cock fighting and his "breed" of special chickens: poison. The autopsied carcasses revealed that they had remarkably high levels of arsenic in their blood, two to three times the lethal dose needed to kill a chicken, which suggested that these chickens had been fed poisoned feed for a long period of time, possibly since birth. Chicken Charlie's game cocks did not have to develop fighting techniques because they were literally poison delivery systems: As soon as their opponents drew blood, instinct would compel the chicken to peck at the wound, and the convulsive death of the opponent would follow nearly instantaneously.

The poisoning of all the chickens, fighting and food breeds, was called ritualistic by the prosecution, who asked the jury whether it was such a stretch to believe that a man who could kill scores of innocent dumb animals would extend the ritual to his own damaged son. The defense pled ignorance, even going so far as to put Chicken Charlie on the stand to claim he did not kill his son, nor did he kill the chickens. He claimed it was an accident, that the chickens must have broken loose and gotten in the poisoned feed and gorged themselves, but the state refuted that theory by showing that the deaths of the chickens were deliberate: the poisoned feed in the feeders that day was of a much higher concentration that their usual feed, and its toxicity could only result in instant death. Only a deliberate hand, the prosecution claimed, could have delivered these victims from their indenture.

And so Chicken Charlie is in jail for the disappearance of his son. We kids are sure we will see Chicken Charlie again, and when he is released we wonder what he will do for a living. Cockfighting is certainly out, and who would trust any food vendor that was accused of poisoning? We wonder if he will change his name, like his son Chick, who now runs with some name that is unpronounceable except to his new family, who howls his freedom in the deep forest gulch of Kipapa. Sometimes in the quiet of the night, when the trade winds have died, and all that can be heard is the ceaseless murmur of the island itself in its perpetual cycle of loss and rebirth, we awake to see, like a reassuring postcard sent from some mythical land where everything surely is better, a footprint in blood-red mud on our steps and the diminishing tendrils of some strong scent, of new earth and male sweat, perhaps, of death and eternity.

THE ICEBOX STAY COMING

My grandmother did not believe in luck. She was more fatalistic than that. She believed in *bachi*, an especially virulent form of fate. She believed that most of the time you worked hard for nothing—no reward—because *bachi* happens. The only thing we could do was "be more sly than one mongoose, more *akamai* than *bachi*." So on the day after New Year's in 1932, the year my grandmother took care of me while my parents made the long sea voyage to Japan to pay respect to my father's parents, my grandmother got her first electric icebox. *Bachi*, we knew, would not be far behind.

The arrival of the electric icebox came as a complete surprise to us, and also to the deliverymen, who found her lane too narrow to drive the truck into. In those days, Muliwai Lane was like a number of small working-class neighborhoods in Honolulu where the streets weren't as wide as they are now, squeezed between the shady *haole* enclaves rising up the Ko'olau Mountains and the heat of the Chinatown plain. Even Muliwai Lane's widest point—the circle at the dead end—could accommodate only three people abreast. Years later, when we grew up and wanted to drive, when streetcars and the city bus became not the godsend they were for our tūtūs and parents because "otherwise got to walk," but an unfashionable annoyance, only then did we relent and roll back our front yards so the city could survey and plot and pave a street, while we cheated our lots to build garages. But before that, when our properties were more approximate—see, over there by the hibiscus that I got as a cutting when I was working for the Foster Estate, come big, yeah, our yard probably ends somewhere over there, and the Wongs', most of that side over there is theirs because, well, what you going do, they always need more room for their growing family otherwise *bumbye* got to put their house sideways, and of course that ditch over there that runs into Muliwai Stream is part of the widow Gonzalez's property because she needs it to drain the wash water for all the extra laundry she takes in—all our front yards spilled together and we kids played in one big yard, our yard, along the length of the entire lane, beneath the dormers of our houses like watchful eyes.

So, of course, the truck wouldn't fit and they wanted to unload the icebox right in the middle of Nu'uanu Avenue, where I'm sure they would have left it because even though they were supposed to deliver on Sundays, they said it was really a gimmick for the store owner and carrying the icebox down the slight incline of our narrow lane was too much work for a Sunday morning. They were explaining how lucky we were to have it delivered this far and not be forced to come down to the store and pick it up, seeing as it was all free anyway, when Shane, my best friend from across the street who always called on me around mealtimes and ate so often with our family that he had his own chair at our table, suddenly interrupted with, "Roller skates!" He dashed off while the rest of us watched the deliverymen wrestle the canvas-cloaked appliance off the bed of the truck and onto the ground in front of us: a shrouded mystery almost as tall as a man. Shane returned with a pair of his steel skates and also a pair of mine that I had thought were lost and barked at the deliverymen to raise the legs of the icebox one at a time, as he expertly slid a skate under each leg and adjusted the positioning of each with the skate key. Soon, a little parade formed down our lane led by my exuberant grandma, high-stepping like a drum major, followed by her new icebox now propped on rattling roller-skate feet beneath its four legs, flanked on both sides by the relieved deliverymen who guided the icebox down our little hill, followed closely by our curious neighbors and their children who had come to witness this remarkable event.

The deliverymen negotiated the icebox down the lane past the Tokina house and the monstrous hibiscus plants that rampaged through their yard, the unfortunate victims of their eldest son's studies in botanical grafting at the university. They took a right at the mountain apple tree onto the path toward my grandma's front door, where they raised the icebox up so that we could retrieve our skates. It was only when the delivery men had mounted the wooden steps for the front door, sharing the burden of the icebox between them, that we realized that the icebox was too wide to go through the doorway. It wasn't as if Grandma's doorway was unusually narrow, it's just that no one had ever imagined a need for a doorway wider than the space it took for one person with groceries to pass through. It would only be years later, after half of Muliwai Lane had been appropriated, when the stream had been diverted and my grandmother's house razed to make way for the looming concrete condominium that threw shadows so large people said the area birds had stopped singing because they had been plunged into a perpetual night-fall, that I wondered how she managed to get some of the other furniture into her house, like her double bed and the couch. I like to imagine Grandma arranging the furniture first and then having the walls of the house built around her, like a queen ant who settles into a new location. If so, it would help to explain why, in fifty years of living in the house, Grandma never once replaced or moved any of the furniture, but kept everything arranged in its familiar place, so that no matter how long we were away or how far we traveled from Hawaii, we would always be able to return to her and the intimate, comfortable surroundings of home.

After some half-hearted attempts, mainly at Grandma's urging, to turn the icebox sideways (even though it was square) and back two of the legs through the door while trying to angle the rest in, the deliverymen put down the icebox, stripped its canvas covering and declared, "Da buggah too big but." They left the icebox facing the street on the stoop immediately in front of the front door, ren-dering that door useless and forcing us to enter the house through the back door in the kitchen, a habit that continued long after the icebox no longer barred the front door, because, by that time, the warmth of the kitchen had become the invitation into our home and the front door an alien thing, so much so that to enter anyone's house through the front door again made us feel as welcome as door-to-door sales-men or proselytizing religious fanatics.

When I think about it now, it seems a strange thing to do, to leave a brand-new appliance outside, directly blocking the front door, but that day as we fingered the engraved brass nameplate that read "Capitol Ice-O-Matic," admired the solid oak cabinet that gleamed like the hull of a newly christened yacht, and winked at ourselves in its gleaming chrome hinges, the icebox no longer seemed out of place, but seemed as if iceboxes everywhere were always placed outside on the steps of the front door. Grandma made some lemonade and gave the deliverymen a drink before they left complaining about more deliveries, and we drank the rest in celebration. Everyone was still gathered around our steps, shaking their heads and laughing, marveling like the proverbial lucky woodcutter who cut down a stalk of bamboo to find it filled with gold coins, when one of the deliverymen came running back waving a paper in his hand and looking for a signature.

He needed the signature of Hadashi Matsuyoshi, he said. Everyone fell silent as we realized that Hadashi had won the "Holiday Dreams" drawing at Lim's

Hardware near Fort Street. Lim's is gone now but used to be located next to the old Chinese medicine place—the one with the gold dragons painted on the windows and bottles of dried atrocities that populated the nightmares of many a Honolulu youth—and around the corner from the Luck and Prosper Culture Club. You always knew when you were getting close to Lim's because you could hear the swearing of the old Chinese men and the castanet clacking of the mah-jongg tiles from the club and could smell the slightly sweet and dusty odor, like a desiccated perfumed corpse, from the Chinese medicine shop.

Every year on the day after Thanksgiving, Grandma would go down to Lim's and carefully inspect the prize—one of the fancy "automatic" washers with a wringer or the newest Electrolux vacuum—before inevitably entering the holiday drawing. "You don't want to appear too da kine," she would tell me, "otherwise next year he going make the prize junk." And because the rules stated "only one entry per person," Grandma took it upon herself to enter everyone in our family separately, including Hadashi, our cat, so named because his stark white legs and feet made him look like he wasn't wearing any shoes and was just "going *hadashi*."

"Hadashi, he stay sleeping," Grandma said, which was what he did every day after a night of feline *holo-holo*. It took him all day to recover from his nocturnal carousing, sleepwalking from one sunlit spot in the house to another, until dinnertime, after which he would disappear and we wouldn't see him until sometime the following morning, sleeping it off again.

"Can wake him or what?" asked the deliveryman. "He gotta sign this."

Grandma shook her head slowly and seriously, as if even the mere consideration of the idea could bring catastrophe. "You went heard the saying, eh: Let sleeping cats lie."

"Yeah?"

Grandma nodded.

"Come mean and everything? What, swinging?"

"Li'dat," she said ominously. "Scratch you up, too. Just like get claws."

The deliveryman gave a low whistle. "He must work late, eh."

"Let sleeping cats lie," Grandma warned. "Gimme, I'll sign for him."

The deliveryman nodded. He took a pen out of his shirt pocket and handed both pen and paper to Grandma. He watched her while she signed. "I thought was dogs. Let sleeping dogs lie."

She shrugged and handed the paper and pen back to him. "Whatevah," she said.

For the next couple of days, everyone in the neighborhood dropped by to get a closer look at our new Ice-O-Matic. It was as big as a regular icebox and append-ed to the top was a large cylindrical object, rather like an oversized hatbox, which Grandma informed everyone was called a "monitor dome."

"Like one brain," she would explain.

The thing she was most proud of, however, was neither the fact that she would never again have to hang the "Ice Today" sign from our front window, which when repeated by our neighbors over the years would eventually shrink the terri-tory of the iceman until he was reduced to the two-block area of the Chinatown fish markets, nor that she would never have the daily drudgery of emptying the icebox water pan again. No, what she was most proud of, what kept her from fill-ing the refrigerator with food those first few days and made her keep only a pitcher of water in there so that when the neighbors came by to gawk and admire she could offer them a glass of water, was the tiny freezer compartment in the corner that made macadamia nut–sized ice cubes that she would drop into her startled visitors' cups while they marveled at the pleasure of having something they never knew they needed: ice on command.

To this day, I don't know if it was the outrageous luxury of having our own personal supply of ice, or if it's just some weakness in human nature that makes us angry at victims of good luck, but suddenly our neighbors, people who were more "Auntie" and "Uncle" to me than my blood relatives, started to avoid us. They no longer stopped their yard work when we walked down the lane but let us pass like strangers. They never asked to hear about the latest twist in the continuing saga of my parents' attempt to break generations of filial obligation by refusing to inherit the ancestral property and instead were trying to convince my father's parents to pass it down to the next eldest son. We no longer got the overflow cut flowers from the Matsushimas, who grew orchids for the florists, and so Grandma quietly re-moved the empty vase from the center of the table. We started to hear mumblings of how Grandma "went cheat the contest," although they had all done exactly the same thing. And during mango season, we no longer felt welcome to the fruit from the Lees' tree, even though that one tree always supplied more than enough for the entire neighborhood, and we had to start buying mangos from Chun Hoon Market like tourists.

The only person who seemed as thrilled about the refrigerator as we were was Shane, who presumed that his brilliant roller-skate idea that first day gave him license to raid our refrigerator whenever he wanted, thereby eliminating the burden of having to wait for mealtimes to eat our food. Hadashi also, the rightful owner, took to his refrigerator right away, and for the rest of his life could be found spending his daylight hours sleeping on the warm monitor dome.

And Grandma, did she worry and fret like I did about our neighbors? Did she miss not getting some of the *tako* that Uncle Shige caught every Sunday when it was still possible to find them along the South Shore side? Did she ever mutter a curse against this *bachi* that equally gave and pushed away in the same motion? Are you kidding? All the tightfistedness and shrunken hearts of our neighbors seemed to make her relish her good fortune even more, and she polished that refrigerator every evening after dinner, in plain sight of everyone in the neighborhood, as if to make manifest her joy of rubbing it in their faces. As we walked down the lane, she boastfully complained even more loudly about her icebox, which she rechristened the "Bill-O-Matic" for the amount it drove up her electricity bill. Whenever I pointed out the latest snub—Mr. Ka'ai burning his yard waste and not offering to burn ours at the same time like he always did—Grandma would just shrug and say by way of explanation, "People come funny 'kine sometimes."

Even weeks later, Grandma would still pause whenever she approached the house and gaze at her refrigerator, with the intensity of an artist studying a still life. She did this often and would sometimes look at the neighboring houses as if to compare the paucity of their doorsteps, unblocked by the latest technology. I would cringe and look away whenever I saw her doing that, for I considered it an ostentatious display, until one day she nudged me as we stood side by side on the path and said, "Look little bit funny, yeah?"

I looked up at her house and tried to cast a critical eye on the comfortable chaos of my childhood home, which, if it were translated to music, would present a cacophonous din. The simple melody of our original whitewashed wooden structure, discordant with the newer addition hastily tacked onto the front to make room for me when I was born, accompanied by the warbling extension in the back that settled unevenly over the years, creating a permanent glissando from its high point near the front door, sliding down through the living and dining rooms where it bottomed out in the kitchen, and finally, imposing itself like a strident countermelody; the new electric icebox that looked exactly the same: standing patiently at the front door like a persistent suitor waiting to be let in, humming as it always did when it was on, with Hadashi sleeping on the monitor dome, as formless as a bag of poi, fitting himself so perfectly to the curve of the unit that one would swear that the icebox had grown hair. "More funny 'kine than usual?" I asked.

Grandma gave me stink-eye. Then, studying the neighbors' houses once again, she said, "I going fix 'em."

She said it with the conviction of an oath. Or a curse. I couldn't tell which. All I could do was hope she didn't mean to get us in deeper with the neighbors.

Which is, of course, exactly what she meant.

One evening, soon after her pronouncement, Grandma led a phalanx of men down Muliwai Lane. In those days even construction workers wore uniforms, and these men in their pale blue uniforms and black boots looked less like gang laborers from Japanese Hospital than an invading force. At their head was a man they all called "Yeah-No," who, I found out later, had been indebted to my grandmother ever since she, as the nurse on duty that night at the hospital, had resuscitated his first grandson after the boy had slipped on a reef while harvesting opihi and been sucked out and spit up face down on the beach five nervous minutes later.

I stayed in the house and watched Grandma marshal the battalion into her front yard where she proceeded to address the men and point to different areas of the house, formulating a strategy for attack. She was barely finished before Yeah-No stepped out of the crowd, turned back toward his men, and issued his commands to them. Some of the men went up the stairs to inspect the icebox, and the rest of them moved to different areas along the sides and front of the house, clearing away debris, moving my Grandma's anthuriums to the rear of the house, and drawing lines in the dirt. Yeah-No circled around the house with Grandma, occasionally stopping to kick the concrete footers of the foundation, as if inspecting an automobile.

Over the next week, mysterious deliveries appeared in our front yard: a couple of torn bags of cement, a load of slightly warped but usable planks, half-empty boxes of nails and brads, even a couple of cans of paint that looked suspiciously similar to the color they were painting the new wing of the hospital. It would be from Grandma that I would learn how to get things done in this world—not by charming the *lunas* and their bean counters, but by befriending the people who actually carried the loads, for they were the ones with the most to offer. By the time the weekend arrived, our yard was choked with misfit building materials.

Early the following Saturday morning, I was awakened by voices and hammering outside of my bedroom window. I knew immediately that Grandma's troops had returned, and so, making as little noise as possible, I rolled stealthily out of bed and onto the floor, where I crawled to the dresser. I pulled some clothes out of the two lowest drawers and changed into them while still lying on the floor, which resulted in my underwear becoming twisted and bunched up around my waist like a sumo belt. But speed was critical, so I would have to wait until later to adjust myself. I snuck out of my bedroom door, and not seeing Grandma anywhere, sped through the kitchen and out the back door, where I ran straight into her backside as she stood on the steps talking to Yeah-No.

"Look who finally went wake up," Grandma said as I got back on my feet.

"Yeah, no," he said.

Grandma looked at me, frowned, and then yanked down my pants. "How come you stay all *kapakahi* like this?"

"Yeah, no," he said as Grandma turned me around and untangled me, "Look like somebody tried to pick him up by his underwears."

"Anyway, good thing," she said as she pulled my pants back up, "just in time for go work."

"Yeah, no," he said. "We need somebody for bring us water."

Grandma nodded. "You go follow him," she said to me.

My escape had proved futile. I had been drafted into Grandma's army. "Okay," I mumbled.

Yeah-No looked at me and laughed. "Going be good exercise but," he said as he led me back out to the front yard.

"Yeah, no," I heard Grandma say.

Fueled by Grandma's massive lunch of miso butterfish, pickled eggplant, pansit, Primo, and poi, and kept rejuvenated by my missions of water, Yeah-No's men finished Grandma's new porch in just one day. It was a splendid porch that was wide enough to turn a horse and ran the entire length of the front of the house. Although the porch shortened the front yard some, it had a large overhanging roof that not only protected her new icebox but also gave us a sheltered place where we could play outside, even when it rained. Even though she now had room to move the refrigerator anywhere she wanted, Grandma elected to leave the refrigerator exactly where it was blocking the front door because as she said, "Going look funny if we move 'em."

Then a funny thing happened.

Mr. Wong, patriarch of his family and the acknowledged "Mayor of Muliwai Lane" for using his crony connections to force the city to bring electricity to our little lane, came by the next evening with his sons-in-law, all six of them, as we sat on Grandma's porch in the new rocking chairs she had bought.

"We seek," he said, "your permission to study your porch." Although he and my grandmother were approximately the same age, his dignified bearing and elegant manner of speech made it seem as if he had come from an earlier, gentler time. Despite what everyone told me, it was hard for me to believe that this man, who seemed the epitome of the shrewd investor with several of his own businesses in Chinatown as well as directorship on the boards of many charitable organizations, had gotten his start as a contract laborer on one of Hawaii's sugar plantations.

"Go," Grandma said to the mayor.

We sat on the porch and rocked while the men discussed the details of the porch construction with each other in Chinese. They peeked and peered under our porch for a long time with Grandma occasionally interrupting them to point out some special feature that Yeah-No had specified: the metal caps that covered the posts in the footings to prevent termite damage, or the tongue-and-groove laths that they used to finish the eaves. When they were done and bowed to her in thanks, she pointed to the stacks of unused material Yeah-No had wanted to burn with the rest of the scrap but Grandma had kept, telling him there might be some use for that yet. "All that over there, extra. Take 'em."

The mayor bowed toward her. "Never mind, you," she said to him, smiling.

Armed with their information and the scrap wood, the Wongs erected a huge balcony from the second floor of their house. It had a generous platform, large enough to land a helicopter, and during the daytime it was commandeered by the growing number of Wong grandchildren, who used it as their base of operations for their neighborhood adventures. But in the evenings, the balcony belonged to Mr. Wong, who had built a raised stage onto one corner of the balcony so that he could perch even higher and not only see the ocean but also smell it. "So we never forget," he would often say when he invited Grandma and me over to share his evening view, "how lucky we are to live here."

Soon afterward, Shane's dad, unemployed for years with a mysterious injury that allowed him to do everything but go back to work, could be seen for a couple of hours each day with a paint can and brush, repainting his house. He worked like an artist should, spending much of his morning studying the blank wall that was his canvas, before slapping on the white paint in an inspired vision, and then lying in the yard the rest of the afternoon to monitor the drying of his work. Even Mrs. Gonzalez, whose yard had always had the severe utilitarian look of a laundry—large vats and sturdy washtub stands networked by the spiderweb of clothesline strung up for maximum drying efficiency—spent her evenings planting a showy flower garden around the edges of her property, which would become our favorite place to net butterflies.

Grandma looked out at what she had done and saw that it was good. "See," she said to me, "What I went tell you? I almost went fix 'em."

"Almost?"

"Not *pau* yet," she said as she watched young Mrs. Ka'ai trying to calm her wailing baby by walking up and down the lane. "There's one more thing you have for do."

I froze. Even my heart stopped to listen. Being volunteered by Grandma was something I never got used to, as the outcome could be as benign as running to the store to pick up some flour or as malevolent as cleaning elderly Mr. Anderson's yard, who, I was convinced, must have been feeding his Doberman other smaller dogs judging by the size of the messes I had to clean up.

"Yeah," she said, motioning to the icebox over her shoulder, "Go give some ice to Darleen."

Relieved, I hurried down the porch with my fistful of ice and offered it to Mrs. Ka'ai. "Here, Grandma said it would help with the baby's teeth."

Mrs. Ka'ai took the ice from me and soon Muliwai Lane grew quiet once again as the baby burbled happily. Mrs. Ka'ai then went up our stairs and sat on my rocking chair, rocking and talking quietly with Grandma. I stayed out in the middle of the lane to watch and wonder about the two of them, Grandma and her new icebox.

Starting from the following day until it finally expired thirteen years later—just quietly stopped humming there at our front door—the icebox became a community resource. No one was refused: Not Mrs. Matsushima who wanted to borrow some space for the *haku* and *lei* for her grandchild's first birthday because they were some kind of special mountain flowers; not Mrs. Cruz who wanted to cool the whipped frosting on the guava cake she made for the church every week; not even Old Man Tanaka who perpetually kept his can of bait in the icebox because "Going make the worms easier to handle."

Only once, years later, when the Ice-O-Matic was long gone and the mystery of electric refrigeration had worn off, so much so that the only time we talked about our refrigerators was to complain about having to clean the frost buildup in our freezers all the time, did I ask her what had seemed obvious to me, even as a child: "Why didn't you just make the door wider?" It would have been so much easier on everyone, I explained, not having to build a new porch and all. I invoked a picture of what that would have been like, of having to go only a few steps to get something out of that icebox, instead of having to go out the back door and around the side to the front of the house, to get, say, a glass of milk.

Grandma stopped rocking and just looked at me. Finally she said, "You never learn nothing, yeah?"

In later years, we could always tell who was getting a new appliance or a new piece of furniture on the lane. The workmen would come one day and chalk lines and arcane symbols around the front door. The next day they would come with their axes and hammers and frame out a new door, leaving a gaping wound in the front of the house like a missing tooth. After the new refrigerator or couch had been delivered the workman would come back and finish the door proper, but we always made sure to make it as narrow as the new building codes would allow, because, as Grandma said, "Sometimes when opportunity knocks at your front door, more better leave it outside."

RELIEVERS

I was tired of losing, so when they shipped Chun Ho's uncle off to Vietnam, I took it upon myself to find us a new coach for the summer to lead us out of the basement of the Honolulu Little League. All spring I had been working on my slider and rising two-seam fastball, and my dream was to walk into ninth grade proceeded by a reputation as an aggressive inside hurler who was ready to bean a few backs and knees when the situation demanded.

I didn't blame Coach Ho too much for our losing record even though some of my teammates did. Although we didn't quite understand what a draft number meant, even on Muliwai Lane in those days, all of us knew that the announcement of another death of a brother, father, or son was just an army-green sedan away. So I held my tongue on game days when Coach would have us close our eyes, turn our faces to the sun and have us imagine it was our last day on Earth, playing the last baseball game we would ever play. "What position would you play on that day," he would ask. Sometimes this exercise was too intense for the younger kids, and I could hear them start to sniffle, but most of us would clamor to play the undeserved positions we only daydreamed about: pitcher, catcher, first base, or shortstop.

As a result, our team specialized in walks since our pitchers could barely throw pitches that reached the plate, in stolen bases since our jittery catchers were afraid of the ball, and in errors since our shortstops were slow of foot and poor in judgment. But if we players were seeing that calamity before us, Coach Ho seemed to be watching another game entirely as he leaned back on the team bench with a broad smile on his face and a dreamy look in his eye.

Most of our fathers were not in the lane that year; some of them, like my dad, were already in Vietnam, and others were working double shifts at the hospital or at the bases to support the troops. No one seemed to have time for baseball except for us kids, and that is why I knew I would have to find a woman to coach our team.

"How about our moms?" Shortshit suggested. Although he was the smallest on the team, he was still our best shortstop. "We could ask one of them."

Dawkins snorted. "What do they know about baseball? They never come out to the games." That wasn't really true, but we overlooked his sentiment because we all knew he hated his mom. She was young so she wore tight bell bottoms with macramé belts and belly-baring t-shirts, and made everyone call her Julie instead of Mrs. Dawkins. She was much younger than all the rest of our mothers, and while that was enough to make Dawkins hate her, for the rest of the team, we were all sort of half in love with her.

"No, we're not looking for baseball knowledge, anyway. We have enough of that already here among us," said Fleabag, our catcher and team philosopher, as he pointed to some of us. "What we lack is someone tough enough to make hard decisions that will turn us into winners."

We all nodded at his sage advice. Could any of our moms be considered tough? There were some, like my family, whose dads were not around and whose moms had to go it alone. But even then, these same moms would later look at us a certain way and suddenly crush us with their hugs while they murmured something about high school and just four years from the draft. We all agreed that this latent sentimentality disqualified them from the tough category.

Someone mentioned Shane's mom, and we all turned to look at him.

His mom had gone from housewife to big boss when she took over the house painting business that Shane's dad had had to abandon when he got arrested and convicted for trying to liberate several cases of liquor from the back of Uptown Supermarket in the middle of the night. But Shane just shook his head. "She paints during the day and cries at night," he said. He looked at his shoes and kicked at the dust. "I think that's all she can handle."

His admission stilled us and we quietly looked away from each other. That's when I saw my grandmother stride out of the lane and jaywalk across the street, gliding along with an orthopedic cane in each hand pumping like a dry-land cross-country skier as she propelled herself into the breach that the rest of us called 7-Eleven.

****

People think I use two canes because I have to. No, I use two canes for speed. You ever wonder why a dog can run faster than a human? Four legs better than two legs. That's why by the time the Boy caught up with me, I was already in the 7-Eleven. Unfortunately, I couldn't see him because the overhead lights in that place had immediately blinded me. I tried to tell him to watch out, that the lights were too bright and that he was too young to go blind, but all I heard coming out of my mouth was, "Augh, augh, augh."

"Grandma! What are you doing?" I heard him say behind me.

I swung around at the sound of his voice and my right cane struck the door frame just over his head. It reverberated in that empty store like a gunshot. "I can't see! I can't see! It's like looking into the face of God over here!"

"What are you talking about?" he said. I could feel him push my back trying to get me further into the store, so I spread my legs and locked the left cane. No way was I going further into that phosphorescent maw. In that brilliant glare, I could just make out the registers, and noticed that the teen clerk had already crouched down and was peering at us from behind the safety of his counter.

"At least get out of the doorway," he said. A second shot was fired as I banged the other side of the doorway with my cane while I was bringing it around. Couldn't he see that the lights were too bright? I tried to jab my cane toward the ceiling but the newspaper rack was placed too close to the door. Somehow, I caught the corner of the newspaper rack which sent it keeling over and vomiting its load of newspapers all over the floor like a drunk.

I could hear the clerk talking to someone on the phone, either his boss or the cops, and before I could bang the doorway one more time and get another shot off, the Boy grabbed me around the waist, pinned my arms to my sides, and wrestled me out of the store. All I could do was beat on his shins with my canes until he released me in the parking lot. Even then, I noticed he stood between me and the store entrance.

"Every week they find some new way to kill me, and you do nothing," I said.

"They are not trying to kill you…"

"Oh, yeah? Why the bright lights this week? They're trying to blind me…"

"All the 7-Elevens are like that…"

That could be true. I hadn't considered that. There was only one conclusion. "Then they're trying to kill all of us."

"Us?" said the Boy.

"Yes, us. All of us old people."

He just looked at the ground and shook his head. It was children like the Boy in front of me that were the problem. If Old Man Tamura had raised his kids right, when he up and died, his kids would have come back from the mainland and taken over his place, instead of selling the entire corner lot to the 7-Eleven Corporation. But 7-Eleven, by bombarding every mailbox in the neighborhood with a coupon for a free half-gallon of milk, was the really nefarious one. How could I get the Boy to understand that the floors of new 7-Eleven were not the sticky comforting floors of Tamura's Superette, but a too-shiny and too-slippery modern substitute that spoke of the Corporation's plot to rid the neighborhood of old people by breaking their hips?

Sirens in the distance seemed to grow louder. "Let's go," he said pulling my arm and leading me out of the parking lot. "Why you gotta wage war with them every week?"

"Because I still want my free milk," said I, shaking my coupon at him.

****

We entered the first week of the season without a coach and to say we lost the first game would be to understate the magnitude of our defeat. Molasses, the slowest player on the team and our first baseman, had forgotten his glove, and so for the first inning, the infield was rolling the ball to him to try and make an out. When that didn't work, I gave him my glove since I was the only other left-hander on the team. But since I was pitching, I couldn't hide my grip on the baseball and the other team was able to read my pitches early and hit me deep into the outfield. Because the outfield was so busy running down fly balls and home runs, our centerfielder Salty Meat started getting sick, so he sat in the grass behind second base and started throwing up the beef jerky he was constantly chewing on. Dawkins and Carter, the remaining outfielders, saw that Salty Meat was allowed to sit down and sat as well, only rising when the ball was hit to them. Only Shortshit at shortstop was able to make any plays, and even then he had to field the grounders and then run down the batters and tag them, because, as he said, "I may be Shortshit but the rest of you guys are just shit."

The umpire stopped the game in the third inning after the other team was up by fifteen, and awarded the win to them because "by the nature of our play" he determined that we would never be able to catch up. The other team volunteered to spot us ten points so that we could continue playing, but Fleabag picked up the baseball, threw it over the fence into the street, and walked off the field. The umpire shrugged and declared, "I guess I'm done here," and left the field as well.

The other team started to pack up their gear, but since this was our home diamond, we just left our stuff on the field and made our way to the water fountain to console ourselves. After I jostled myself into a respectable place in line at the water fountain, someone said, "Hey, Lefty, isn't that your grandma?" and we all looked to where he was pointing.

Sure enough, there was Grandma, wading out into the busy four lanes of Nu'uanu Avenue. Like the sea parting around Moses, cars stopped suddenly around her as she slowly crossed over to the far gutter to retrieve Fleabag's angry baseball before waving it over her head at us and making her way back. Stillness gripped Nu'uanu Avenue until Grandma hoisted herself back onto the sidewalk, and then the cars roared back to life, flooding the avenue with motion once more.

We watched Fleabag join her at the sidewalk and then engage her in a lively conversation. I knew the only reason Grandma had gotten the ball was because she couldn't stand to see anything go to waste, even if it was a game she really didn't understand. Still, her conversation with Fleabag seemed to go on longer than any I had ever had with her, and when she handed the ball over to him at the end of their conversation, I could swear that they also shook hands.

Fleabag walked over to the water fountain where we had all gathered, and cut to the front, where he pushed Shane off the pipe. He bent his head down and took a long draw before turning his head and geysering it back out over Shane.

"What the hell, Fleabag," Shane said as the water streamed all over his head.

"Why do we always drink this," Fleabag said, "It's hot, it's gritty, and tastes like iron. It's like drinking coffee grounds from a manhole cover." He wiped his mouth on his sleeve, turned around, and let us have it. "Well, boys, I found us a coach."

Just then, I could see that Grandma was not walking home, but had veered toward us at the water fountain. "No," I said. "No, no, no."

"Yup, yup, yup. Your grandma," he said pointing at me, "has agreed to coach the team for the rest of the season."

****

By the time I got there, the Boy had crumpled over as if someone had kicked him in the groin, "Oh, God," he groaned.

It was a brilliant idea, but when I looked around, the team looked as puzzled as puppies at obedience class. I couldn't believe it: not one of them could see the potential of this pairing.

"Look, guys, she's perfect. She's just what we need," said Fleabite. He looked at the Boy who was shaking his head like a fighter recovering from a body blow. "Just ask Lefty."

The Boy looked up like a cornered animal. It was the same look he gave me that time I found those dirty magazines under his bed.

Fleabite sighed. "Have you forgotten, Lefty? Your grandma is an expert on hopeless situations and turning them around, right? That's what my mom told me."

The Boy nodded. At least he couldn't deny that. So Fleabite explained to the team how before they had all been born, I had been a babysitter who specialized in taking care of kids whose mothers had just died. I would usually swoop right in after the death of a young mother and stay with the family for about nine months or so, by which time Dad and the kids could usually hold it together. "Mom told me that a job like that might weaken a person over a time, but Lefty's grandma seemed to draw strength from it. All those years, she would work from family to family, propping families up and putting lives back on track." He turned towards the Boy to address him directly. "And what are we, if not a hopeless situation?"

"This team could use someone who knows their way around bringing the dead back to life," I said.

A short boy started nodding and pounding his glove and the rest of the team soon followed. The team started pounding the Boy on the back, but nothing seemed to dislodge his gloom. "I don't understand," he said to me. "What do you get out of it?"

"This," I said, and hit Fleabite in the chest with the back of my hand. Dust rose from the chest piece where I hit it.

"Oh, sorry," Fleabite said. "This thing is pretty dirty." He started pounding his chest and years of dust started rising from it like puffs of smoke. Everyone backed away from him except me and the Boy. When he was finally done beating himself up, we were all covered in a veil of smoke like demons just summoned from the underworld.

Later that night, the Boy eyed me up at dinner. He thought I didn't know that he didn't want me to coach his team. What he didn't know is that I didn't really want to coach his team, either. I knew losers when I saw them. But that fat boy's equipment was a wondrous thing. "What's that fat boy's name on your team?"

"Which fat boy," he said.

"You know, the one with the equipment."

"Fleabag?"

"Yeah, that's it." Even though he had a lousy nickname, that kid drove a hard bargain. "How come he's the only one who gets to wear all that?"

"He's a catcher, grandma," the Boy said. "All catchers have to wear that equipment." I watched him shovel more food on his fork and throw it back into his mouth. Even when I cooked for all those unfortunate families, the appetites of teenaged boys always amazed me. Where did it all go? Not to their brains, I thought. "You know," he continued, "that's why you shouldn't be coaching our team. You don't even know what a catcher is."

"I do."

"What?"

"The catcher," said I, "is the one who catches the ball."

"From who," he said accusingly.

"From the thrower, obviously."

"The pitcher, you mean," he sneered.

"That's the problem with your team, too many pitchers, not enough throwers." When I was a nurse, I got tired of patching people up and sending them back out into situations that were now worse than when they came in. Sure, I could help them while they were at the hospital, but many times the real challenges were still waiting for them at home. That's why I became a substitute for the dead, showing those families that sometimes you have to fend off life for a little while before you can move forward again. Fixing things and letting them go when they were ready was far more rewarding. "Your team could use a little more raw energy and a little less by-the-book."

He shook his head. "You know, Grandma, I'm the team's pitcher."

I nodded my head like I knew that. "That's what I mean, you and Fleabite out there, thinking all these thoughts, these baseball thoughts, instead of just going out there and letting your enemy know you know what's going on and you're here to vanquish them and win." I banged the table with my fist for a little emphasis and caught the end of the fork. It flipped end over end in a slow arc over the table before the Boy grabbed it in midair and returned it back to the surface. "Maybe there is hope for your team after all," I said.

He snorted out a laugh. "Whatever, Grandma. Just remember that as coach you need to be there in the park when practice starts at three thirty."

"Every day?"

"Every day."

****

I could tell that the team didn't know what to think about the old lady coaching. She didn't run practice like Coach Ho. Sure, she was there, but Fleabag spent most of the first practice explaining baseball to her. I mean, when I walked behind them to get a drink from the water fountain, I could hear him explaining real basic stuff like outs and walks and hits. Then, at the next practice she didn't want to talk to anyone, not even me. Fleabag offered to work with her again and even I tried to get a few words in, but she waved both of us away like annoying mosquitos. She watched us the entire time, and I don't mean with the bored expressions the parents watched us with, but like a cat who watches a bird for twenty minutes before pouncing and tearing it to pieces.

The whole time I thought, how is this supposed to make us better? She didn't offer us any suggestions, didn't say anything when we made some boneheaded mistake, and definitely had no advice when we went up to bat. But all practice long, for almost a week, she just watched with those steely eyes of hers, taking it all in like a prison guard minding the cons. Then on Friday, after our last practice before our second game, she sat us down to "make a few announcements."

First, she pointed at Shortshit with her cane and said, "This little kid here is the only one who is in his correct spot. So he will continue to play Shortshit."

"I'm Shortshit," he said to her.

"I know," she said, "that's what I just said."

"I'm Shortshit," he said again pointing to myself. Then he pointed out to the field. "And I play shortstop. Short. Stop."

She rolled her eyes. "Whatever." Then she turned to the rest of the team and waved her cane at them. "The rest of you are all playing the wrong positions. I don't know who told you kids that you should be playing those positions but come Saturday all of that is going to change."

Stunned silence was followed by an immediate uproar. Rather than being alarmed, the old lady seemed to enjoy it and basked in it like high praise.

"For example," she said as she pointed at me, "This one here, my own flesh and blood, will be moved from the throwing mound to deep center."

I was stunned. I was clearly the best pitcher on the team. Before I had a chance to say anything, though, ex-centerfielder Salty Meat asked, "What about me?"

"You, Salty Meat, have no arm to speak of. Out there, you can barely throw the ball back to the infield," she said. I guess she was paying attention. Although Salty had speed, she was right about his arm, he threw like an off-balance duck. "So I'm moving you closer to the action." She pointed to second base. "Maybe over there by the middle base."

We all looked at second base and then at each other. I looked to Fleabag for objections, but he was nodding his head. "Well, at least you'll be closer to second base in case you need to throw up again," he said to Salty Meat.

Cries of "where am I playing, where am I playing" rose from the team but Grandma just raised one cane like a conductor's baton and motioned for silence. "All will be revealed tomorrow," she said, "all the changes."

"Except for me, Shortshit," he said. "Right, Coach?"

Coach nodded and winked at him. I glared at him but he said, "I think this old lady knows what she is doing. At least she got one thing right."

****

One thing about baseball, too many goddamn rules. I still didn't know anything about the game, even though that kid Fleabite spent a day trying to explain it to me. At the end of the day, I figured if he knew the rules so well, maybe I should focus on something else. So, I moved everybody around, what else was I going to do? They can't keep doing the same thing and expect something to change. Sort of like with that damned 7-Eleven. All my neighbors agreed that the floors were too slick, the lights too bright, the music too loud, etcetera, etcetera. But they said they didn't know what to do. Really? They didn't know what to do?

"We have to take the fight to THEM," I told the kids before the game.

The Boy, who was miserable since I took him off the mound, scoffed and said, "What does that even mean?" I don't really blame him for being upset, but really, I was tired of him tracking that mud and dirt from the mound onto my porch. Let someone else deal with that for a change.

"We get out early, we score some points," I said.

"And we don't look back," said Fleabite. I was beginning to like that kid more and more.

So the start of the game got delayed because I couldn't tell the two haole boys apart. You tell me, two tall white boys with short hair and ball caps, and I was supposed to figure out who was who? It was like I was seeing twins out there, Dawkins and Carter. I just had them play next to each other in the outfield so I could keep my eye on them. It wasn't till after the game that I figured out that Dawkins was the one with the hoochie mother but by that time it was too late.

Watching the game was an education. The armor that the catcher wears seems pretty impervious to any kind of knockabout. Balls in the dirt bouncing up and banging into the shins, direct shots to the chest, even a few ricocheting off the helmet, that Chinese boy didn't even cry once. I had him play catcher so I could learn how to don the armor. Every inning Fleabite had to teach him how to put it on: First, shin guards strapped up in the back, followed by the chest protector over the head and cinched on the sides, and that glorious helmet over the top. By the third or fourth inning, I knew that I would have no trouble getting it ready for my needs this coming Sunday at the 7-Eleven. I was even thinking of uses for that round padded glove he was wearing when the game seemed to end.

"Okay, we didn't quite win this game," I said to the boys after it was all over. "But this time at least we got to finish the game."

Some of the boys nodded their heads, but some of them seemed skeptical. The Boy, especially, looked dismayed. "When fighting a faceless enemy, sometimes you lose the early battles before you figure out how to win the war," I explained. "So what do we do? We pick ourselves off that cold, slick floor, check ourselves for injuries, and finding none, we vow to return next week to battle again."

More boys nodded their heads now. "Yeah, no one got injured," said Molasses.

"That's because you dodged practically every hard hit that came your way at third base," said Shortshit.

"At least he moved," said Shane, "when he was playing first base, it was hard for him to even bend down to get the ball."

We all agreed that movement was an improvement for Molasses. More boys stepped up and offered that Salty Meat did not throw up this time, Fleabag seemed less itchy since he moved to first base and was out from under the catcher's equipment, and even Shane suggested that he was better for the team at pitcher, because "pitchers aren't expected to hit well" and he had a natural talent for missing the ball with his bat.

By the time they left the field, things were looking up; at least the team left with a better attitude than the one they came to the field with. Only the Boy looked downcast as I made him carry the catcher's gear back to house so I could clean it up and remove the teenage boy stink.

****

My breakfast was ruined when Grandma stepped into the kitchen wearing Fleabag's gear. She looked like a scarecrow in slipshod armor, as if the whole thing was conspiring to pull her down to the ground. She strutted into the kitchen, the shin guards flapping against her legs creating a ripple of applause every time she walked. Her face was radiant inside the catcher's mask and her eyes sparkled with new vitality. It was like she had been elected queen of a Costume Ball for the Insane.

"Well, what do you think?" she asked. She turned to give me an eyeful and I noticed that she had managed to tie the round catcher's mitt to her hips, like a leather bumper for her backside. "Of course, I'll be holding the cane in this hand," she said as she held up her right hand.

"Umm, I…"

"Yes, eyes. I'm well protected there." She swung her cane up toward her face where it hit the mask and bounced off, leaving a delicate tone in the air. "All I need now is a shield for my other hand."

"A shield?" I suddenly imagined my grandmother as the lone samurai in all those Japanese movies I had seen, surrounded by a circle of bad guys as she battled each of them to death until she was the last one standing. In a 7-Eleven. "What do you need a shield for?"

"To get milk," she said, waving the coupon as she skipped out the door.

****

I found the perfect shield on my way out the lane, sitting there on top of Old Man Wong's trashcans. I grabbed the handle of the metal trash can lid and held it in front of me. Light, not too smelly, and not really my concern if it gets a little smashed up. Who's going to notice? Old Man Wong was in his nineties and could barely see anyway.

I had to admit, that fat boy's helmet was a little too big for me, so my head rattled a bit inside of it. I couldn't really look up either, so it made it hard for me to see the traffic light. But that didn't seem to matter because as I approached the corner across from the 7-Eleven, the traffic seemed to slow down and stop for me. There was a kindred spirit in one of the cars because I heard him say to his companion, "That's why I don't go the 7-Eleven anymore," and I raised my cane and shield in agreement with his assessment of the dangers that lay ahead of me. He gunned his car engine in affirmation.

I crossed the parking lot and straightened my fanny protector before stepping onto the automatic doormats. The door opened with a hiss and a blast of frigid air-conditioned air tried to bowl me over. I put my shield up and pulled the chest protector tighter around me and fought back this wintry attack, making my way to the sales counter. Again, the group of people at the counter stepped back, awed by my outfit and sense of purpose. The young man behind the counter stared at me. I lowered my helmet to protect myself from the bright lights and battled his wordless challenge with my own formidable gaze.

Eons seemed to pass as the tick-tick-tick of the Slurpee machine metered out the time. Finally he broke down and said, "Ma'am, is there something you need?"

I scoffed at his attempt to belittle me with his "ma'am" putdown. "Milk," I growled.

With a shaking hand he pointed to a row of refrigerator units at the back of the store. Shiny metallics and bright colors sang their siren songs from behind the glass doors, trying to distract me from the solid sheet of ice that was the floor. The lights above reflected the unforgiving white glare here and there. I slapped the coupon on the counter. "Challenge accepted, little man," I said.

As I moved forward across that frosted wasteland—cane forward, then shield, cane forward, then shield—my confidence began to grow. Just then saxophones began to wail from some music just above me, but I ignored their distracting dirge and continued on my perilous journey. When I reached that refrigerated gateway, I could see the half-gallons from every species eyeing me—two percent, skim, even the heavy whipping—but I opened that portal and grabbed me a whole. The smoothness of the carton surprised me, and I tucked it into the crook of my left arm behind the shield for safekeeping. Its heft, I figured, would give me comfort on my journey back.

I blame the Boy for what happened next, for as I was about halfway back to the counter, a full three-quarters of my mission complete, the entrance doors slid open I saw him bound into the store and look wildly around. The minion at the counter pointed his shaking hand toward me, and just as the Boy saw and started advancing in my direction, the floor beneath me began to shift. Already off-balance on my left side from my half-gallon load, I felt the world starting to tip so I swung my arms out for balance and prepared for ground impact.

****

The next thing I saw was an explosion of Pringles as Grandma's cane beheaded a row of cans on the shelf, followed by the lifeless thud of the half-gallon of milk hitting the floor. The trash can lid flew out of her hand like Captain America's shield, and she slowly turned and bounced on the carton of milk, which erupted in a fountain of milk all over the candies on the lower racks, before she hit the floor in a clatter of catcher's gear, milk, and Pringle shards.

For a moment, none of us moved, dazzled by Grandma's performance. It's only when the clerk whispered, "Is she dead?" that we came to our senses. I rushed over to the aisle and rolled her over. Her eyes were closed and I started to think the worst. I heard the clerk on the phone, calling for an ambulance. I patted her down beneath the equipment, feeling for broken bones.

"Quit feeling me up," she growled, as her eyes snapped open. "I'm not one of your floozy girlfriends."

"Oh, thank God," I heard myself say, much to my surprise. Grandma raised herself up to a sitting position and started to struggle with her helmet. I unsnapped the straps in the back and took it off her head.

"Everything was fine till you got here," she informed me. She gazed at the chaos around her. Rivulets of milk escaped from the aisle, carrying boats of fake potato chips along with them. "If it weren't for you, I would have made it."

The sirens approached loudly and suddenly cut off. There was a bustle at the door as the paramedics wheeled in a gurney before reaching me and pushing me aside. I stepped back and watched my grandmother sit in a pool of milk and calmly answer their questions. I even found myself feeling a little proud of her as she slapped their hands away as they tried to remove the shin guards and chest protector from her body.

"This is the only thing that saved me," she told them. "You think I'm going to take this off?"

The paramedics retreated and lifted her onto the gurney, milk-soaked equipment and all. I led the parade of onlookers into the parking lot as they loaded her into the back of the ambulance.

"Don't forget my coupon," she yelled from the ambulance before they closed the doors. "It's still on the counter."

****

On Monday, instead of practicing, the team came to visit me in the hospital. Some of them stood around the bed with tears in their eyes. "This is why you guys always lose," I told them. "You're too soft."

"I didn't know something could stink so bad it could bring tears to your eyes," Salty Meat said.

The short one seemed especially broken up; he was crying so much, he had a hard time breathing. "Don't worry, Shortshit, the girls here are taking good care of me." I patted his hand. "I'm not going to die."

"We might," he said, "if you don't get rid of that equipment. "

It had been twenty-four hours since the incident, but I was still wearing the catcher's equipment. It was so rank from spoiled milk that I was afraid the staff would take it off and throw it away, and then where would the team be? Instead, I kept the chest protector and shin guards on, and hid the helmet under the bed. A couple of times they sent the head nurse to come talk to me, but I remembered her as a candy striper from my working days.

"Pansit, if they can't stand the smell, just have the nurses move to the station further down the hallway," I told her.

She shook her head and laughed. "Okay, but my name is Priscilla, remember. Just because I'm Filipino doesn't mean I'm named after food."

"I know you need this for practice," I said to Fleabite as I pulled out his helmet. The way he drew back, you would have thought I had pulled out the head of the opposing pitcher.

"Uh, no, you can keep it," he said. "That smells like roadkill. I don't think we can wear that anymore."

"Keep it?" The Boy said, accepting the helmet. "We have to get all of it out of here."

His words seemed to get the team going, and they began to remove all of the rank gear. I felt like a skinned animal as they removed the heavy outer layers till there were just bones underneath. They piled it all on top of the Boy, who wasted no time getting it out of there. As he left the room, I could hear the nurses clapping and cheering as he walked past their station.

****

As I left the hospital with the soggy gear, Fleabag suggested I just shitcan the whole mess in the dumpsters by the parking structure, but I told him that I had a better idea. I led them like a putrid Pied Piper from the hospital to the 7-Eleven, where I stepped inside the store and dropped the whole mess on the floor in front of the counter.

****

I had been home from the hospital for only a few hours when 7-Eleven sent a freckled-faced young man with red hair to the house to make up with me. I wasn't going to let him in the house, so he pleaded with me from the porch.

"A lifetime's supply of milk," he offered through the screen door. He never said it, but I could see it in his eyes and the way he fidgeted. They were afraid of a personal injury lawsuit.

"Why would I want that?" I asked him. "I'm lactose intolerant."

He looked at me and frowned. "Why were you using a coupon for free milk, then?"

I closed the door in his face. "If he doesn't understand why people like free stuff, I can't help him," I told the Boy.

A succession of young men came to the house but each seemed stupider than the one before. They offered me free lifetime delivery services ("Goodness, you mean from all the way across the street," I said before closing the door), free cigarettes ("I quit smoking decades ago, are you trying to kill me?"), and even a free 7-Eleven-emblazoned vehicle that they drove up to the house ("If that car is designed like your stores, you really are trying to kill me.") Each of them left empty handed until they sent an older woman in high heels who told me that she was the "Corporate Counsel."

"Is that supposed to mean something to me?" I asked as I closed the door.

Corporate Counsel stuck her foot in the doorway and the door bounced off her expensive pump. "Only that I am the boss and am authorized to make any deal I need to," she said.

I think it was her foot rather than her words that made an impression on me, but I considered Corporate Counsel again. "There's nothing I need from you," I said.

"We need a new set of catcher's equipment," the Boy said from across the room.

"New catcher's equipment," I told Corporate. I watched her write something onto a memo pad. "Make sure it is an extra large, it needs to fit a fat boy."

"Done," Corporate said, "what else can I do for you?"

I looked at the Boy but he just shrugged. Then he said something useless like a lifetime's supply of soda or some nonsense. "I'm tired of coaching those losers. Maybe you can get them a real baseball coach."

"No problem," she said as she scribbled. "We can sponsor them, get them new uniforms, find someone to make sure they aren't an embarrassment to the brand."

"Yeah, yeah, yeah, whatever. That's enough about them," I said, "Here's what I really want."

****

Turns out that what Grandma really wanted was sticky floors, dim lighting, and silence. Basically, what they used to have in Tamura's Superette. The two ladies haggled like vendors in Chinatown and Grandma eventually settled for changes at the corner 7-Eleven: Rubber mats on the floor in high traffic areas, a free pair of prescription sunglasses, and Japanese music played between the hours of one and three-thirty p.m., the hours most likely for Grandma to shop. "After the wretched single men who had to buy their lunches at a convenience store and before the damn after-school kids," she told Corporate Counsel.

Our new coach was actually pretty good, but since he didn't come from the neighborhood, he was a lot like 7-Eleven: mainland-born and sort of distant. He must have had a real name, but we called him Coach 7-Eleven and he didn't seem to mind. We even managed to win a few games, although I never got back on the mound. Grandma would drop in on the games sometimes, and I would see her sitting in the stands smiling and shaking her head. I like to think she was shaking her head in wonderment rather than disappointment, but she always left before the last inning so I never found out.

The ceasefire agreement with 7-Eleven Corporate lasted the rest of her life. While she didn't live long enough to see us kids from the team graduate and go our separate ways, whether that be draft mandated or volunteer, she would have been proud to know that I did earn a reputation as a centerfielder with a cannon for an arm that served me well during my tours of duty; that Shortshit continued to not grow and was found lacking by the Review Board; and that her favorite, Fleabag, became a bulkier backstop during his high-school playing days and used that experience to shield his squad mates during an attack and came back home to be buried as a hero.

THE SUMMER OF
MIRACLES AND LIES

That summer, my mother and I were living with my Grandmother in Honolulu while Dad was with the army fighting the war in Vietnam. At least, that's what I told all the kids in the neighborhood. The truth is that he was stationed in Thailand, working a noncombat position maintaining a communications infrastructure for the air force and its pilots. He had only recently been commissioned—one of the air force's "thirty-day wonders" who had been rushed through officer training school in thirty days rather than the usual ninety—and shipped off to Southeast Asia to fill the vacuum in the line officer hierarchy. I could have boasted of the intelligence that allowed him to work in the heavily abstract and highly mathematical field of electronic communications; I should have been proud of his sense of duty and patriotism that drove him to volunteer and serve during the entire conflict. Instead I repeated my lie when needed and remained quiet when a drafted brother or uncle came back full of rage at their "greenhorn lieutenants" or the "zoomies who didn't know what it really meant to fight a war."

I was happy living with Grandma, not only because as her only grandson, I was indulged in ways that baffled my mother and rendered unrecognizable the strict disciplinarian who had raised her, but also because Muliwai Lane seemed a world away from Hickam Air Force Base, where everyone—the teachers, the grown-ups, even the other kids—could talk only about the war. On Muliwai Lane, I could take off my silver P.O.W. bracelet without guilt, bury it in a corner of my sock drawer, and go outside to find some adventures with my new best friend, Christopher.

Christopher was the same age as I was, and at thirteen, we ruled the lane. It was our last year in power—we would be entering high school that fall—and if Joy and the others before us were any indication, as soon as we entered McKinley High, we would stop associating with the younger kids and start worrying about records, clothes, and our hair. Because Christopher was Grandma's neighbor, I had known him all my life, but it wasn't until I actually moved in that we became fast friends. As a young child, Christopher was often absent or bedbound, the victim of an aggressive and insidious form of leukemia that seemed to roar up every few years only to be battered into a seething remission by increasingly larger doses of radiation, drugs, and luck. His frailty, coupled with my grandmother's constant and graphic updates, had rendered Christopher into something other than a kid like myself. He became an observable process of pity and fear, like a maimed insect flailing in a glass jar.

But I soon learned it was everyone else who projected these things onto Christopher, for he himself saw strengths where others saw weaknesses: his physical weakness meant that his brain was stronger. He did not live a life punctuated by sadness and sickness, but lived for the ever-increasing pursuit of fun. And the pity that was shown to him by grown-ups was just a propaganda tool to keep kids thinking about themselves, and not thinking about creating the kinds of mischief that Christopher was famous for: placing Grandma's plastic fruit centerpiece in the freezer and putting the frozen strawberries in the back of the cupboard so that a month later Grandma discovered it by the trail of ants that were traversing in and out of her cabinets. Even after she permanently banned Christopher from her house, he told me, "You know, I think deep down she really enjoys it." In short, he was the perfect companion for a thirteen-year-old boy looking to ignore the names, numbers, and funerals of war.

The only times the war was unavoidable were the infrequent phone calls from my father in Thailand. The calls were a kind of theatrical performance on both sides: He with his false gaiety and "no worries" prattling that belied his true nature, cautious and responsible, and me under strict maternal orders that the best thing an officer's son could do was cause no worries for his father. Everything that came out of my mouth that summer was either a lie, half-lie, or omission. So when he asked about my team, the baseball team that he had coached every season before the war, I made up statistics for nonexistent players and asked for his advice on my slumping batting average instead of telling him that his absence had sent the team into disarray and eventual abandonment. Soon we would both run out of things to lie about, and he would end by telling me to be good and more helpful to my mother since I was "the only man around the house." It was at that moment I would be tempted to mention the man who lived in Grandma's backyard.

It is unthinkable these days to allow an unrelated person, almost a stranger, to live in your backyard, but on Muliwai Lane in those days, it did not seem so unusual. For while my grandmother legally owned a square plot just big enough to contain her house, her hibiscus hedgerow, her coffee can–potted anthurium stands, and the rusty washing machine she kept outside that we kids had nick-named "squeaky-leaky," in reality, very few of us lived on our "legal" plots. The paths of our lives refused to be curbed by property lines, and so Grandpa Wong appropriated space from his neighbor on both sides to keep his six daughters, their husbands, and his seven grandchildren under his ever-expanding roof, the Matsushima boy parked his car under Auntie Emma's mountain apple tree and could be seen ferrying the widow to her downtown doctor appointments for the rest of her life, and my grandmother had become caretaker of a strip of property that protruded from one corner of her backyard like the state of Florida. It was on this little peninsula that the man lived, in a buckaloose old gardening shed that smelled perennially of sweet lime.

There were a number of rumors about the old man, whom we kids had named Calamansi for smelling like the Filipino lime. Even then I knew that the seeds of truth about his background were probably far more mundane than the fanciful offshoots that grew from them, but I hoarded the rumors anyway, col-lecting the private mythology that would sustain me and the other kids on the lane. The Hawaiians claimed Calamansi had been high-born; then, through some mysterious betrayal they would never utter, saying that to repeat is to relive, Cala-mansi had been exiled from his family and community and now lived in disgrace under the pity of my Japanese grandmother who did not understand such things. The Japanese suspected that Calamansi had once been the Hawaiian contact for the Tokyo Mafia, "a sort of evil tour guide," they said, "for the people who really made Japanese history." Then, during the yellow-peril frenzy just after Pearl Har-bor, Calamansi had turned to the authorities and squealed on all his cohorts, from whom he was still hiding out. The Chinese swore that as a young man, Calamansi had once been a cop on the Chinatown beat, where he fell in love with a hostess whom he tried to rescue from her madam. He tried humanitarian reasoning, then bribery and flattery, and when none of that worked, he used the blunt instruments of authority and the law to shut down the house. But when he went to find the girl, he found her in her room, hanging from the ceiling. "She was the victim of the madam's spite," they would say, "and now he hides from her ghost."

The person who should have known the most about Calamansi, my grand-mother, refused to answer any questions about him or the reason why he was living in our yard. The most she would say was, "It's *giri*," an emotional obligation. She left it to me to imagine the favor that Calamansi had once performed for our family in the time of my grandfather, the specifics of which had been long forgot-ten, but whose heft was still important enough to be borne by our family.

The only thing I knew for sure about Calamansi is that he would perform small miracles if you brought him a suitable offering. For simple feats like restor-ing an ancestral vase the parents had brought back from the old country that was broken playing living-room baseball, a bag of Leonard's Malasadas, still hot, was all that was needed. While we anxiously looked at our watches and waited, pray-ing that he would fix the vase before our parents came home, Calamansi would savor the malasadas leisurely before asking for all the vase pieces and disappearing into the shed. He would emerge from it hours or minutes later, vase completely restored with no telltale cracks, with just enough time for us to run home, place it back on the table or shelf and rush out the door before narrowly missing mom or dad coming up the steps. More complex miracles demanded greater offerings, generally things that money could not purchase, like the labor of our little gang of seven- through thirteen-year-olds hauling twenty-five-pound bags of plaster and lime from the street where the deliverymen had dumped them, back to the shed where Calamansi piled them in a corner for the production of spectacular and fanciful shells that he sold to tourists in Waikīkī. All of this in return for the invisible manipulations that made once steadfast parents mysteriously relent in their objections to getting a dog, or the surprising need for overtime work that was demanded from parents on Muliwai Lane on the exact day report cards were to arrive in our mailboxes.

The one thing he would not do, which was the only thing that the adults ever wanted, was to bring back the dead. Their offerings reeked of their grown-up misunderstanding of his powers: gold watches, rare whiskeys, or chattering par-rots with ribald stories. He refused them all, saying with an apology that he could not use his talents to undo that on which God had final judgment. So the adults left cursing and questioning the worth of a conjuror who could only perform parlor tricks for children and not bring back the one thing money or love could not purchase.

Shunned by the adults in the neighborhood, especially by my mother and grandmother, who never invited him into the house and never offered him a meal or even uttered his name, Calamansi kept a schedule not unlike Hadashi, our cat—sleeping through most of the day, rising in the afternoons to disappear from the lane, and returning sometime during the night so that we kids could always find him sleeping on the platform in the shed that served as both his bed and workbench. It was here on an early May morning in the summer of 1972, while Calamansi slept like a sun worshipper, his face turned toward the heat that poured through the shed's only window, that I blackened over his window with a blanket and waited for the darkness of the false evening to prod him awake.

Calamansi burst out of the shed as if it were on fire and lurched blindly a few steps before clotheslining himself on Grandma's empty laundry lines. As he lay on the ground, he said that he had been dreaming that a warm-blooded fat woman was trying to kill him. At first, he felt lucky that a long-haired, dark-skinned wahine of big bones and ass was bringing him drinks in a teak bar on Hotel Street, "just like before time." Things were going good when she suddenly sat on his lap and pressed her lips hard against his, "and then it was like drowning in shallow water. The weight and heat of her body was everywhere, choking me."

He shook his head. "Hoo, must be like what happens after you die," he said. "You think you're in heaven when whammo! Hell happens!"

As his eyes adjusted to the light, he sat up and spied the army blanket I had thrown over his window. "So it was you and not the devil who went put her into my lap."

I nodded. "Dad sent me that blanket," I said. And then, stupidly, "From the air force… in Vietnam."

He nodded at my lie and I turned around to peel the blanket off the window, using exaggerated movements to squelch the guilt rising like nausea within me. "Look, I need you to…" I started again. "I need a miracle."

He shrugged and started toying with a file of ants. He crushed the last one with his fingertip and then started drawing lines in the dirt, the ants following obediently. He led them into a spiral where they congregated in the center. "Try watch," he said as if I weren't already, and then he made the ants do something I had never seen before or since. He lined them up and marched them out of the spiral backwards, abdomens leading, heads following like tails, and for a moment it was like watching life in rewind, the ants returning to their starting place as if no time had passed.

"It's a big miracle," I said. I handed him the invitation I had received that morning.

Calamansi pulled the invitation from the envelope and read it over. He worked some saliva over in his mouth before spitting a wad that broke like napalm onto the ants, scattering them in all different directions. "What are you offering?"

I just stood in front of him until he realized that I was offering the biggest thing I could think of: Me. Myself. My labor.

"No," he said as he handed the invitation back to me. "What am I going do with you?"

"I can help you," I said, "with stuff."

"Stuff? What stuff?"

"Well, I know you make shells…" Calamansi just shook his head and looked away from me. "And I can help you with your work at night."

Calamansi started like I had pricked him with a needle. "What do I do at night?"

I didn't know. "I can do anything," I said, and then thought about the rumors: con man, gambler, pimp, hit man. "Except kill somebody. I don't want to do that."

Calamansi started to laugh, but it quickly died out when he saw I wasn't joking. He squinted at me. "How is a ten-, twelve-year-old going to help me?"

"I don't know how a ten-year-old would help you either, but I'm thirteen now…"

"Ahh…"

"And I have lots of skills. Plus I like to stay up late."

"I see…"

"And anyway, it's not about me." I shook the invitation at him. "It's about helping Christopher."

Calamansi thought about that. "I no can help him. What you're asking… looking for… impossible."

"No it isn't, not for you."

Calamansi didn't say anything. "We have to make this deal," I said holding up the invitation. "Grandma would want us to."

I had blindly played the trump card, hoping that using her name would resound as loudly within his history as Calamansi's name resounded in ours.

Calamansi rolled his eyes and stomped off a couple of steps, muttering unintelligibly. As he mumbled to himself, he shook his head occasionally, as if to erase some image from the Etch A Sketch of his mind. Finally, he sighed and walked back over to me. "I want to make it clear that I no can do anything," he said, "but I can try help you."

"Okay."

"No, too quick. If you like work with me you need to open your ears." He leaned closer, and his breath soured his usual lime scent. "Our deal is: if you try help me, I try help you."

"Okay, I get it," I said, impatient with his grown-up restatement of the obvious. "That's what I want."

Calamansi nodded wearily and said, "Good, then do two things for me right now: one, no more waking me up by sending a fat wahine in my dreams to kill me."

I handed him the blanket. "Done."

He took the blanket and then pushed my forehead back with his palm. "Two, no bother me, I like go back sleep. *Bumbye* meet me here in the afternoon."

I turned to go.

"Hey, you good with numbers?"

"Numbers?" I thought about the school year I had just finished and how I spent much of it flailing around in the deep end of long division before drowning in a wave of percentages and powers. "You mean just numbers? Sure, I can handle numbers."

"Good," he said as he turned around to leave, "otherwise you would have had to handle the killing."

"Where the hell have you been?" Christopher said when I finally made it to the gymnasium of Sacred Hearts Academy.

"Wouldn't you like… the hell… to know," I answered shakily. It was our swearing summer, where we finally tried to put into practice what we heard all of our lives from our fathers, uncles, and coaches. We tried to increase our familiarity with it, practicing our diction on each other—"You ASShole, You assHOLE, YOUUUUUU asshole"—but Christopher suggested that we had better start incorporating it into our daily speech if we wanted to be proficient for high school, where we needed to stand as peers among the other potty-mouths.

"Hell what?" Christopher said as he lifted the screen out of the gymnasium window. "That was weak, man."

I ignored him as I jimmied the window open and then helped him through it, shoving behind with a little more force than necessary. He landed on the other side with a thud and a chuckle.

"I want you to be the first to know," Christopher said as he watched me climb in through the window, "that I have officially turned girl crazy."

Christopher often chose our early morning raids on the gym to try out some pronouncement on me. It was part of our daily ritual that summer, rising early and slipping into the Sacred Hearts girls' school gym, borrowing a basketball from the equipment room to play a few rounds before the advent of our closing ritual sometime between nine and nine-thirty: a broom-wielding math teacher with sideburns like steel wool who chased us out of the gymnasium, swinging his broom and spouting a stream of profanities.

"It's about time," Christopher continued. When he got no response from me, he added, "It's something you should think about."

"You're soooo full of shit," I said, returning with a basketball.

"Hey, that was much better than that other thing you tried to say." Christopher reached in and tried to steal the ball from me. "You may end up a man, yet."

I let him steal the ball and drive toward the basket before I ran after him, the first part of my response drowned out by the bouncing basketball and our drumming feet, leaving only the "…you!" echoing in the gym as we both stopped to witness his wobbling shot from the top of the key.

We always started with a couple of rounds of straight one-on-one that I would win, and then he would grow tired and start tweaking the rules, changing the emphasis of the game by weaving elaborate basketball fantasies where talent and height mattered less than imagination and daring. We started talking more and shooting less, so that a winner was decided not on the basis of the score, but who had had the most memorable shot that almost made it or who had concocted the most unbelievable basketball scenario—like his contention that these early morning practices were necessary to keep up his game so that when Meadowlark Lemon came looking for an opponent in Hawaii, Christopher would be ready with his Kalihi Islandtrotters. Somehow, Christopher always bested me in these matches, and it allowed him to maintain his theory about us and sports: I, the brute, the clod, the proto-human knuckle dragger, would of course excel in situations that demanded only the basest of the human capacities: sweat and guts. Whereas, he, Christopher, master strategist and student of the sport, excelled in the higher-function activities that required grace and finesse, like leadership and motivation on the court. It was a good theory, and one that we had planned to use in high school when we tried out for the JV team as a package deal.

"Just stick with me," he would say as we sat at half-court, having abandoned the pretense of physical activity all together, "and I'll get you on the team."

"What are you talking about," I would counter, rolling the ball to him. "I'm the one getting you on the team. You need to stick with me."

"Ask any coach, brains are far less common than brawn."

"Yeah, but brains aren't going to put points on the board."

"See, typical muscle-headed misunderstanding," he would say, and we would spend the rest of the time sitting on the floor, rolling the ball to each other, comfortably rehashing the old familiar arguments until the arrival of our hairy, broom-brandishing timekeeper Quixote.

We always spent the rest of the morning and on into the early afternoon together, wandering the island like young regents surveying our domain. We rode the bus to the North Shore and posed as phony tour guides at the Dole Plantation as we led groups of tourists out into the pineapple fields, encouraging them to "pick their own" and then collecting their tips as we escorted them directly to the parking lot, bypassing Dole security. We went to Waikīkī to ogle the blondes in bikinis and laugh at the young servicemen on R&R learning how to surf from "Steamboat" Sam, our hero for blazing a career track from former professional wrestler to Waikīkī beach boy and lu'au crasher who was welcomed everywhere he was, or was not, invited. We hung around Ala Moana shopping center outside of Sears to chat up groups of pretty Japanese girls using a broken Japanese made up mostly of Japanized English words—"date-o" for date and "cute-o" for cute, for example— and a smattering of schoolyard Japanese, generally crude terms for body parts and body functions that always brought a giggle and the occasional invitation to lunch. And when we were really bored, we'd walk down to Hotel Street to watch the Filipino street preachers—"rrrrrrrrrrepentaaaaaa"—and cheer on the transvestite street walkers trying to pick up lonely servicemen.

By then, Christopher was usually tired, and we would retreat back to the lane for his "siesta," an inescapable fixture in his life since he was a toddler. After leaving his house, I would return home to lull myself to sleep on Grandma's porch by secretly envisioning myself as Christopher's defender, dispatching the legendary bullies of high school: Junior Faamoe, rough but easy to confuse; Dee Fukui, whose wicked tongue could be shut down with a return volley about her precocious acne; and Carl the rumor monger, who had no follow-up to the honest "Yeah, so what" defense. I felt ready for bullies and naysayers of any sort and every provocation, but I hadn't counted on Christopher's parents, whose challenge, issued through the invitation of a Christmas party in July, spoke of their certainty that he wouldn't make it to the end of the year.

The real hard work began after my siestas, where I was Calamansi's captive for the rest of the day and into the night. At first, he had high hopes for me in the fine art of phony shell making, the goal of which was "to create the shells God like make but didn't have time." If that were true, then God had taste as bad as the tourists in Waikīkī. Out of his workshed, Calamansi produced monstrous shells of paste that could have housed small dachshunds and were decorated in the tastes of the time:

a "hippie" model with small colorful sunburst decorations that vaguely resembled flowers and peace symbols and hung from a macrame sling imported from the Philippines; a gilded "disco" model that looked like gold for two weeks, until the acids in the paste tarnished the brass foil into a muddy black; and for the R&Rs at Fort DeRussy, a "military" model, which, depending on the way you tilted the shell, would show either subtle shadings of red, white, and blue or striations of green and black camouflage.

He liked to brag that creating his concoctions "required the steady hands of the surgeon, the knowing eye of the artist, and the cold capitalist heart of the sugar planter." But after three days, when he saw I had the hands of a stevedore, the eye of the colorblind, and as much capitalist heart as the cowardly lion, he ended our lessons by recommending that I continue studying hard in school, maybe becoming a lawyer or CPA, because, clearly, it just wasn't in the cards for me to be useful to society.

Instead, we turned to his nightly pursuits, where with a "Here, carry this," I was thrust into an alien culture holding a black, beat-up guitar case. It was a familiar case, the one Calamansi carried with him every time he left the lane but no one had ever seen open, and so in our Bonnie and Clyde–fueled imaginations, we supposed it held the tools of his trade: sniper's rifle, handguns, and the hit man's handy garroting wire. Every night after dinner, I would sneak out of the house carrying the case that held his well-worn twelve-string guitar tuned in the *ki-ho'alu* slack key style and accompany Calamansi on his walk to Chinatown, where we caught a bus to Waikīkī. Somewhere on that bus ride, Calamansi tensed up, cracked his fingers, licked his lips, and by the time he reminded me to be sure to get him some cigarettes when we got off the bus, I knew Calamansi was long gone and that I was now the protégé to Tiki: Waikīkī session player and tourist maven.

Our first stop was at the Ilikai Hotel, where we waited for a legitimate employee to enter through the service entrance before slipping behind him and following him through the kitchen to the livery corner. We would pick our favorite shirt off the rack, the green and white aloha-print ones the Ilikai used for its breakfast service, because they were the only ones that did not have "Ilikai" emblazoned on them but carried a stylized "I" which Tiki told tourists was a "T." A pair of white slacks looked best, so if we could find them on the catering staff rack we took them along with some white shoes, though usually we had to settle for the black ones. Thus attired, Tiki would have me follow him as he strolled through the kitchen toward the emergency exit, studiously avoiding the maître d' and head waiter while joking and kidding with the cooks as if he known them all their lives: "What, braddah, couldn't find older fish to serve than that? And you, what, that chicken looks so tough I bet it graduated Waianae! Ey, all these pineapple tops no waste 'em. *Bumbye* I going sell them to the tourists as Hawaiian toothbrushes!" Then out the emergency door, and one step to the left to the *lei* stand where Tiki would pick up his red double-carnation *lei*, the de rigueur identity badge for all island entertainers, and with a peck on the cheek to Auntie Alice who always worked the *lei* stand, he would say, "Just bill the Ilikai VIP account." He would then be off to his first gig, me following behind him with the guitar case banging against my legs.

As we got closer to the Coconut Lounge in the Tahitian Lanai Hotel, Tiki would stop more and more often to talk to tourists, pose for pictures, and maybe sign an autograph or two, which only drew bigger crowds of curious passersby who did not know who he was but recognized the uniform of an island entertainer. Occasionally I would be asked to pose for a photo as well, which I'm sure ended up in photo albums all over the mainland as "a cute Hawaiian boy" or "Tiki's son." However, my main job at these gatherings was to collect cigarettes. I would position myself at the outskirts of the crowd to find the particularly anxious tourists to whom I would casually mention that Tiki had forgotten his cigarettes in the limo and how I had lost the money he had given me to buy them from the vending machine, and that was all it took for them to offer me some of theirs. For a cigarette or two ("singles" or "doubles" Tiki and I called these tourists), I would take their hand and push my way close to, but not inside, the closest circle near Tiki, enough to get an autograph or picture after a short wait. The "packs" got the VIP treatment: my personal escort to Tiki himself, where I interrupted whatever he was doing to introduce the person by name, and after a display of aloha where Tiki treated this person with the hugs and back-slappings of a long-lost relative, I would offer to hold the camera and take a picture of the whole group. I sometimes wonder how these pictures turned out, focused as I was on the act of taking the picture rather than the end product, and I shudder to think of all the feet and legs or decapitated lopsided surprises these tourists received from their film processors.

When I had collected enough cigarettes to last through the night and into the following day when Tiki became Calamansi again (at least two packs), I would signal Tiki by putting the guitar case near his feet. By this time, the crowd was generally starting to peak, which was the perfect time for Tiki to announce that he was playing again at the Tahitian Lanai Hotel and that "all you good folks can buy me drinks there." With a good-natured chuckle they let him go, and I again followed him down the street until we got to the Coconut Lounge where Kui Kanaka and the Island Heart Troubadours played nightly.

Tiki, along with "Feets" Funai on the steel slide guitar and drummer "Curly" Leong, made up the Island Heart Troubadours. Onstage, their easy rapport with

Kui made the audience think that the entire group had all grown up together, when in reality, the Island Hearts were all just subjects of the despot Kanaka. Kui Kanaka was one of the many Don Ho–type entertainers at the time, the twenty dollar alternative to the Polynesian Palace's fifty dollar Don Ho's Polynesian Revue. Instead of thirty pretty Polynesian dancers, you got one, Sistah Lani K, Kui's on-again, off-again okay-looking girlfriend. Instead of glass tumblers with Don's visage and his trademark "Suck 'Em Up!" you got white plastic cups with a palm tree and the words "Aloha—Drink More Beer" printed on them. And lastly, instead of Don you got Kui, who early in his career wrote a never-remembered song that made it to the B-side of one of Don Ho's 45s, and thereafter spent his entire life yearning for the acclaim that he felt due to him by emulating Don Ho's vocal characteristics and persona while cultivating the only talent that in any way approached Don Ho's: his capacity for drink. Despite all this, the shows were quite well attended, owing mainly to the availability of last-minute seating in the Coconut Lounge for the procrastinating tourists who had waited until they were actually in the islands before trying to make reservations for Don Ho.

"We have a saying in the islands: There's no one more tyrannical than a second-rate Don Ho," Tiki repeated to whoever would listen. The show ran under Kui's strict specifications, from the tunings of the instruments down to the scripted "ad-lib" banter and affectionate kiddings. Even the take at the bar, and the real reason Tiki wanted me along, reflected Kui's sense of self-importance. Twenty percent of the house cover and bar take was supposed to be split equally among everyone in the group. In reality, Kui got ten percent, his girlfriend got nothing ("in deference to the band," Kui would say), and the three musicians would get three and one-third percent each. It was this compound percentage that confused the musicians every night, who, although they did not know how to calculate the exact amount they should be getting, knew that the sum of the musicians' take should equal the amount of Kui's take, which, before I became the auditor, it never did.

My job was to sit through the first performance, the seven-to-nine-p.m. set, and immediately after the first encore, work with the bartender to count up the cash drawer. Then as the musicians hung around the bar after the performance, I was to bring my prodigious mathematical talent, honed by years in the Hawaii public schools, to bear upon the division of the take. I had one hour before the next set at ten p.m., and it usually took me the greater part of that hour to get everything right. On the bar, I would create two equal piles of money, and let the musicians decide which pile they wanted. Once they picked their pile, I would divide theirs into three smaller piles all equal. The musicians would rotate turns regarding who got first pick, and in this way of piles and picking, the veracity of the method was beyond question.

After that, Tiki always sent me home, walking me back out through the lobby, motioning for a cab, and making sure I was safely in before giving me all of his take and turning to the fans waiting outside for the second show of the night. The band's drinks were usually subtracted from the take for the ten-to-midnight show, and anything left over would be held under the bar and mixed in with the first take of the following evening for my division. All that cash usually excited the cab drivers, and I always promised them a bonus if they could get me back to Muliwai Lane before ten o'clock.

As soon as they dropped me off at the top of the lane, I was all speed. I cut through the Matsushimas' yard to the back, where I raced behind all of the houses on the lane till I got to Calamansi's shed. I opened the shed with the secret code (a sticky door that would only open with two kicks to the bottom, a yank on the door knob, followed by a couple more kicks) and located what Calamansi called the "First Hawaiians' Bank," an empty seashell. I poured the coins in, stuffed the bills in as far as they would go, and then I was back out of the shed kicking the door shut. Before going home, I detoured to Christopher's house and looked through his window to find him asleep before finally stumbling up the stairs of Grandma's porch to go to bed. I imagine my neighbors must have put away a tidy amount collecting the only evidence I left behind of my nocturnal adventures: a scattered trail of quarters, nickels, and dimes.

It didn't take long for the late nights and daybreak basketball sessions to start taking their toll, and, by late June, I was regularly skipping our morning basketball at least two or three times a week. As the weeks went on, Christopher never said anything, never mentioned how he sat outside the gym on those chilly mornings waiting for me, waiting every day for one and then two weeks until I finally showed up one morning, the first time in two weeks, to find Christopher gone, tired of rising early for no reason. And so I slunk back to my bed feeling guilty but also relieved.

We still met at ten to begin our daily assault on the island, but since Christopher no longer exercised in the morning, he wanted to draw our afternoons out later and later. After a morning of indulging Christopher's self-proclaimed "girl crazy" status by closely observing and rating the swimsuit models at the McInerny's Swimsuit Fashion Show and Tea, in which the large group of mostly older women in bright white clothing and large summer hats routinely turned around to glare at us as we discussed notes in the back of the room, he suggested that we take the bus to the North Shore and jump off the edge of the monstrous rock in

Waimea Bay, something he had always wanted to do.

I shook my head. "We'd have to take the Circle Island bus and it would take us forever to get there."

"So what?" he said as we walked toward the bus stop. "It's not like you have anything better to do."

"It's gonna take hours to get there and back," I said, "not to mention the hours it will take to convince you to get your chicken-ass to actually jump off the rock."

"No way, man, I'm ready."

"Yeah, small man, big dreams." We were at the bus stop. "Maybe some other day. I gotta be back home by three."

"Why? What's so special about three?"

"Nothing." We both watched the Circle Island turn the corner and approach our stop. A group of lobster-baked tourists stood up from the bench and started to line up. "I just have things to do."

"What kind of things?" he asked. The bus pulled up and Christopher got in line.

I moved off to the side. "Nothing, just some stuff."

"Doesn't sound so important," he said as he climbed into the bus. He blocked the door with his foot. "Hold on," he told the driver.

"Forget it."

Christopher just looked at me. "What is wrong with you?"

"Nothing, I just have something to do, okay?"

"First, you ditch me and the basketball thing…"

"Look…"

"Then, you chicken out for some lame…"

The bus driver's horn cut us off. "Make up your mind! Coming or going!"

Christopher looked at me. I looked away and noticed that the other people at the bus stop were watching us intently.

"God damn it," Christopher said and stepped off the bus. The bus roared away from the curb. Christopher looked angrier than I had ever seen him, angrier even than the time we were messing around with his father's car and I somehow released the emergency brake, sending us rumbling across the lawn, tearing down laundry poles and part of the front steps before coasting to a stop. "God damn it!"

I folded my arms across my chest. "What?"

"What's going on with you?"

The people were still watching us, so I just shook my head and turned to leave. "Never mind, I just have to go."

I started walking to the other bus stop, the dark, crummy one used mainly by the locals catching the downtown bus home. I could feel Christopher's eyes burning into my back for a few seconds before I heard his slapping feet behind me and a hand wrenching my shoulder from behind, spinning me around.

"Here we are," he spat, "in my last damn year…"

"Shut up! You don't know that." I could feel the anger rising up in my chest, clenching my fist. "I'm not going to feel sorry for you!"

"Everybody says so. My doctors, the oncologist your Grandma had sent over from Kapiolani Children's…"

"No one knows that!"

"Even my parents…"

"Fuck your parents!"

The ferocity of my response surprised me, but it had come from an anger deep inside me, pressuring up like magma ever since I got that invitation, exploding in those words that had bypassed my head altogether and channeled straight through my heart, leaving behind only heat and the pounding of blood in my ears.

We were both silent then, Christopher just nodding his head for a while as we stood in the parking lot. "My parents," he said quietly, not looking at me, "My parents are just… parents."

I knew I should apologize, but I was still shaking and said, "They don't know what they're doing!"

"It's not their fault. They just want…"

"Shut up…"

"They want to give me something…"

"Shut up!"

"They think the Christmas party…"

"Shut up!"

"They think it will make me happy!"

He started crying then and it surprised me. I realized that I had never seen him cry before, not once during the times I went to see him in the hospital, not once at home when he was recovering from the sickness and pain of radiation therapy, not even during Brian's Song. I wanted to hug him, to tell him that they— his doctors, his parents, everyone—were killing him. That I believed and because I believed, I had sacrificed our mornings and now this afternoon in order to work for him. I wanted to tell him about the deal, about how I was working for Calamansi and how all of his powers were working to save Christopher, so that he wouldn't have to have this stupid Christmas party in July but he could celebrate it with the rest of us later. I wanted to say all of this but I didn't. Something, some primordial instinct developed over millennia to protect the fragile emotions of men, descended over my heart and rendered it bulletproof. All I could do was look at Christopher and say, "I'm going home, and you go home to your parents and your goddamned Christmas in July. But don't expect to see me there or get a Christmas present from me until it's really Christmas."

I left him there by himself. Just as a couple of days later, when the entire lane was celebrating an early Christmas at Wo Fat Chinese Restaurant, complete with Christmas trees and carols by the Honolulu Boys' Choir, I abandoned him again.

The whole lane was mad at me. Mom grounded me until I apologized to Christopher and his parents. But it didn't matter. Mom left for her job at the diner in the afternoons, and with Grandma still working her shift at Kuakini, I was free to slip out of the house and join Calamansi. Her grounding had only succeeded in keeping me from seeing Christopher, something I was sure Christopher didn't mind.

All through those afternoons and evenings I worked for Calamansi, not once did we ever mention Christopher. I knew that Calamansi would work his miracle as long as I held up my end of the bargain, so I never refused any of his requests, no matter their legality. I drew buckets of water from nearby Nu'uanu Stream to mix with the lime for his fake shells. When he ran out of sand, I jumped on the bus to Magic Island Beach and stole buckets of the white manicured sand that was strained of cigarette butts and trash by a special tractor every night, and I tried not to meet the skeptical eye of the bus driver as he drove me back home with my filled buckets. When Calamansi needed cigarettes, I went to the 7-Eleven where the teenage part-timers would sell them to me, or if the old lady was working, I would walk further uptown to Iseri Gas Station and use the vending machine on the side of the building before Old Man Iseri could catch me. Even though Calamansi never bothered to check, I never shortchanged him, always bringing back the exact change. I was the perfect assistant and had never worked so hard at anything in my life, which was why I was surprised when I showed up to work one afternoon and Calamansi said that he didn't need me anymore.

"Why? What did I do?"

"You didn't do anything," he said without looking at me as he sat at his workbench. "That's the problem."

"What?"

"You never go to the Christmas party..."

"That doesn't matter," I said. "Anyway, you're out of water." I took the empty bucket and started out the door.

Calamansi stood up and grabbed the bucket handle like a leash. "Christopher is having a birthday picnic tomorrow afternoon. You go to that."

I turned to look at Calamansi. "His birthday's not till November."

Calamansi nodded. "It is at Kawananakoa Park around lunchtime."

"How do you know?"

"He, Christopher, went tell me."

"When?"

"This morning? Last night? I don't know, was still dark out." The look on my face must have registered the surprise I felt inside because he continued, "You think you the only one that can wake me up when he wants something? Besides, you stay coming back here every afternoon and think he doesn't notice?" He swept his arm toward Christopher's house. "It's his backyard too."

Calamansi yanked the bucket from my hand and sat back down. "He said it was his idea. He's only inviting people that he likes, not all his relatives like at the Christmas party."

"I'm not going."

"Ey, he's doing this for you, you know," Calamansi said. "You should go."

"Doesn't matter," I said. "I'm not going."

Calamansi suddenly looked serious as anger creased the furrows between his eyebrows. "You go tomorrow. I don't want to see you here. Ever. You're *pau* here."

"Why should I?" I retorted, hot and defensive. "I'd rather be here, working for you, working for something good, instead of giving up like everyone else!"

"*Pau*. Over."

"What about the miracle? You promised! You promised to keep him…" I couldn't say the words.

"I no can do that, I told you I couldn't do that. No one can," he said gently. He sighed and turned his head to look out the window. It was a typical Hawaiian summer afternoon—the heat of midday had finally dissipated, leaving the cool trade winds to beckon us out of our houses.

"Then what was all this?" I gestured around me. "Was I just some sort of slave? Bring me this, get me that, here carry this… you're just some sort of phony aren't you? Just some… damn phony!" I started to cry. I didn't want to, so I tried to hold it in and ended up sputtering like an old well pump.

Calamansi looked at me for a while, then held my arms down to my sides, leaning into my face. I could smell that familiar scent of limes and last night's drink on his breath. "Ey, I promised to help you, and maybe I should have tried harder. Should have explained more, yeah, but I'm not a teacher. I thought if you hung around enough you would see."

"See what? See how to con cigarettes from tourists? See how crappy musicians can trick tourists?"

Calamansi just nodded his head for a while before speaking. "I don't know much, but the one thing I learn is the life you live is the life you make," he said. "You come to me so worried about a future you no can control… all I like do was make you see that the present stay right here." He was tapping me on the chest. "That we live in the present."

He went on, but I stopped listening to him. Calamansi turned out to be a grown-up just like every other grown-up, and suddenly I felt alone, isolated as Christopher must have felt that afternoon I left him standing in the parking lot. "At least until his real birthday in November," I begged. "That's all. Just four more months…"

"I failed," he said, and then firmly, "Go home. Go home to your mother and grandmother. You no see me here anymore."

I stumbled out of his shack and went home. When Grandma came home from work a couple of hours later, she could tell I had been crying. She was so alarmed she made my favorite dinner, misoyaki butterfish, but even after dinner I still couldn't tell her why.

I awoke late the following day and, defying my indefinite grounding, slipped out the back door to Calamansi's shed. He was gone. All that was left were the bags of lime stacked in the corner, a few half-finished shells, and the army blanket I had given him folded neatly on one corner of his workbench. I sat on his workbench, eventually stretching out and dozing off, wakened only by my mother's calls. I let her go on every fifteen minutes or so for a couple of hours, winding up her anger and waiting until she well inside the house before I answered each summons by throwing one of Calamansi's shells against the shed wall where it exploded with a "whoomp," showering the room with seashell petals as brittle as eggshells.

When the calling ceased and my name stopped reverberating in the neighborhood because my mother had gone to work, I stepped out of Calamansi's shed with the blanket under my arm and walked up the lane and down Nu'uanu Avenue until I reached Kawananakoa Park. It was long past noon, and I could see the adults picnicking at the top of the hill, which meant that the kids were in the back. I hiked around the hill to the far side of the park, where the kids from Muliwai Lane were taming the playground equipment, drumming out their vitality on the structures of steel. Christopher, however, was sitting away from them, in a chair that flared like a mirror in the sunlight, and he waved at me once as I made my way over to him.

"What's with the wheelchair?"

He shrugged. "My mom's idea."

I nodded. Nothing more needed to be said. I could see the uselessness of the wheelchair and could imagine the fights Christopher must have had with his mother about it. We both knew that with parents, sometimes it was just easier to humor their inanities.

"What's with the blanket?"

I shrugged. "My dad's idea."

He nodded.

I walked around his wheelchair like I was going to buy the thing, kicking the tires, releasing the brake, toying with the foot rests, and rooting through the pocket on the back of the seat, while Christopher prattled on about where they bought the wheelchair, a medical equipment surplus place on King Street with fake arms and legs hanging on the wall in different shades of brown from *haole* to Hawaiian, like a menu for cannibals. We both stalled this way until I could stand it no longer.

"Look," I said, interrupting him, "I should've…"

"Ah, it's okay."

"No, I mean, I really… about the… well, everything…"

"It's all right."

We both looked at each other for shorter than a heartbeat before turning away simultaneously, but in that vulnerable sliver of a second, more passed between us than I have said in a lifetime of talking to others I have loved.

"I'm sorry."

"I know."

I smiled. I dared not look at Christopher's face, but I could feel that he was smiling also. "You know," I said, as I unlocked the brakes, "I bet this thing goes downhill really fast."

We spent the afternoon learning what all wheelchair users know: that the large wheels are stable but virtually unmaneuverable at high speed. Much to the consternation of Christopher's mother, I treated the wheelchair as if it were my own, spending the majority of the time in it except when we took turns dragging the chair back up the hill. Just when we started to tire of it, Christopher discovered that if you momentarily grabbed one wheel while flying downhill, the chair would execute a complete 180, sending you downhill backwards. We burned the skin off of our palms, first the right hand and then the left, before we were forced to give that up as well.

We abandoned the wheelchair at the bottom of the hill after our last run and walked toward the playground, nursing the burns on our smarting hands. I could tell he was tired. Every couple of yards I would nudge him with my shoulder or pretend not to see his leg shoot out in front of me, and one of us would fall, pulling the other down with him, until we were both sitting on the ground, cursing and laughing. We carried on this way, taking about half an hour to cross the twenty yards past the playground to the baseball diamond, where we sat leaning on the chain-link backstop.

"Remember the first day you moved into your Grandma's house?" he asked.

"Yeah, what about it?"

"I brought you here," he pointed with his thumb at the backstop. "Remember?"

I remembered it well. Sitting on the top rail together, looking out over the neighborhood for the first time, contemplating the scale of the streets surrounding us: wide Nu'uanu Avenue, an old street that ran almost a straight line from the mountain to the ocean, and busy Liliha Street with its traffic from the foreign embassies, bakeries, restaurants, and hospitals, framing Muliwai Lane into an isolated corner, a one-outlet escape from the din of Honolulu. "I remember you made me climb to the top of this thing, dragging your heavy butt with me the whole way up."

Christopher chuckled. "So what are we waiting for?"

We jostled each other into a standing position. "I'll go first," I said, and as soon as my skinned hand hit the naked steel of the chain link, a shock went through me that made me suck my breath back in and brought tears to my eyes. "Son of a…"

Christopher sat back on the ground, holding his stomach and laughing, "You should've seen the look on your face!"

"Ha, ha, very funny."

"Your eyes," he continued, "they were big as hubcaps!"

"Okay, tough guy, you go first then."

Christopher shook his head and pushed himself up, still laughing. He touched the chain link gingerly. "See, wimpy, no problem." Then he adjusted his grip and started to pull himself up.

I pushed his rear end up until his other hand had a firm grip and then I too gripped the backstop carefully. After the initial shock, the metal felt like ice in our palms, and like juggling an ice cube, as long as we kept it moving, the burns did not have enough time to cause us pain. We scrabbled up the backstop like a couple of pistons, me shoving his rear every once in a while when he seemed to slow down. When we got to the top, we just sat on the rail and looked around for a moment.

"Do you remember what you said the first time you were up here?" he asked.

"Yeah, I said the view was worth it."

"That's right, and I said…"

"And you said that the view from the top is always better than the view from the bottom."

"That's right," he said approvingly, having finally trained his dim-witted puppy a new trick. "That's something I learned a long time ago."

I turned to look at Christopher, but he had turned his attention toward the top of the hill. We watched his mother stand up and shade her eyes as she searched for Christopher among the rabble on the jungle gyms, and not finding him there, scanned the whole area till she noticed us on the top of the backstop, where she did a half-jump of recognition and frantically waved her arms up and down.

I waved back.

"That's not what she means," he said.

"I know."

Christopher waved back too.

We watched his mother kick his father until he stood up and looked to where she was pointing. After motioning us down and our wave back, Christopher's mom and dad started walking down the hill.

We watched them for a while before Christopher said, "I guess we better get off this thing before they get here."

He started to climb down, always an easier task for him than climbing up, so I didn't even think anything about it and focused on getting myself down until I heard him say, "oh-oh." I looked down to see Christopher's hands falling away from the backstop as he leaned back with his eyes closed and fell backwards to the ground in a slow, graceful plunge. I sprang from where I was and landed hard next to him.

Christopher opened his eyes. "I guess that was dumb."

"Uh-huh," I said and picked him up in my arms. The back of his head was dirty but not bleeding. I started to carry him toward his running parents.

"Don't put me back in that wheelchair," he said.

"Don't worry, I won't." I adjusted my arms to cradle his weight better, leaning him against my chest a little more. I remember wondering if he could hear my heart hammering against my ribs, when I suddenly felt a warmth spread across my arms and travel up my chest.

Christopher groaned.

"Ah, it's okay," I said. I could smell the piss on my shirt and feel it running down my arms.

"No, I'm really, I mean… about everything…"

"It's all right."

I looked at him and smiled.

"I'm sorry," he said.

"I know."

I handed Christopher over to his father, who I had never thought of as a strong man until that moment, and he took Christopher and started running toward the parking lot. I ran behind them but couldn't keep up, so I yelled out, "I'll meet you for basketball tomorrow morning!"

"I'll be there," he said.

I stopped to pull off my shirt and watched as Christopher and his dad receded into the distance as they ran up and over the hill, Christopher swinging his legs as he bounced in his father's arms.

Then Christopher died.

I'm not sure what time, exactly. They probably told me but I don't remember. I do remember wanting to close his eyes because no one should die with their eyes open, and I tried to explain that to them, but no one would listen, no one would do it. I only wanted to get over there to close his eyes, but they started to panic, the nurses saying they must have quiet in intensive care, and I started thinking that the problem was that death was too quiet here, and maybe I told them that and they answered that they couldn't understand me when I yelled, so I pushed ahead and they tried to grab me and pull me away, telling me that I was endangering the lives of the other patients, and I think I told them that everyone's life was in danger so what made those patients more important than him, and waiting for an answer while I pointed out this patient and that patient and all the damned patients except that patient with his eyes still open and again they took it the wrong way like I had yelled at them so I moved them out of the way to get to his eyes, but they fell over like they had been pushed and maybe I accidentally knocked over a cart and a tray of medicines but those must have been in the way as well and I certainly did not kick it across the room like they said, and they did not need to call those two men with the broomsticks, because I would have left had they just let me close his eyes, and I tried to tell them that but everyone seemed to have forgotten about him and were turned toward me and that is when I might have started raising my voice asking why it was so easy for everyone to turn their back on him, why was it so easy to forget him now that he was dead, and I tried to make them see, to make them turn their damn heads around, but those two men wanted only to look at me, blocking my way to his eyes, advancing slowly and crouching their way forward like they were stalking a wild animal, forcing me further and further away, and when I tried to explain it to them that I only wanted to close his eyes, and couldn't they see how important it was that no one died with their eyes open, they sprang forward with their sticks, one of them catching me in the chest and the other in the gut, forcing me backward one last time, my shoulder blades touching the corner walls, and that was when I could read their plastic nametags, Zinc and Jake.

It was dark by the time I left the hospital and I was grateful for it. I needed the darkness to blot out the neighborhood so that I could return to home in a black tunnel, seeing only my feet plod in front of me like a blindered horse, and not see Christopher in everything that I had taken for granted on Muliwai Lane. I made it to my front porch, where I sat myself on the side away from Christopher's house and looked out over Grandma's anthurium stands, where I tried to think about nothing.

Sometime later, mom and grandma came out to try and say something to me but I was tired of talk and kept my back to them. They eventually retreated but Grandma came out a minute later with dad's blanket and draped it around my shoulders. I don't know how she got it, but I was glad and pulled it around me. I didn't want to fall asleep but I had discovered that sight was the only reliable sense, the only one I could turn off, and eventually the darkness overtook me.

I was awakened by the smell of burning limes and raised my head to see Calamansi sitting on the porch, smoking and watching me.

"What are you doing here?" I asked. "I thought I was never going to see you again."

He shrugged. "I heard about…" he paused and took one last drag from his cigarette before flicking it off the porch where its glowing end cartwheeled into the darkness. "I thought you might need me."

I shrugged. "Why would I need you now?"

Calamansi nodded as if he understood. "Come," he said as he picked up his guitar case. "We go."

So I left with him, the blanket still draped over my shoulders as we walked out of the lane into that limbo of time where the phrases "late night" and "early morning" lose their meaning, and we entered a city where the ghosts of one day lumbered homeward and the dreams of the next began their slow awakening. We stopped at a line of taxicabs waiting for tired whores and intoxicated servicemen at the corner of Merchant and Hotel, where Calamansi argued with the drivers until he showed them that he had enough cash to get us where we needed to go.

Even then, we had to listen to the cabbie complain all the way out of Honolulu about how this trip was costing him more than it was worth because he would miss the "GIs and their ladies," who always tipped well. It wasn't until Calamansi promised to pay double the fare that the driver quieted down and I fell asleep in the backseat.

To this day, I still don't know where we were when we stopped and Calamansi shook me awake. As I stumbled out of the car and Calamansi handed over a wad of bills to the driver, all I could see in front of me was a solid tangle of hibiscus bushes, pandanus trees, and vines of strawberry guava, like the overgrown gates of paradise. Once the cab pulled away, all light was gone, and we were blinded by a pitch black that surrounded us. Since I couldn't see where I was going, I followed Calamansi's voice, which kept repeating, "There used to be a path around here somewhere, there used to be a path around here somewhere," as Calamansi felt the vegetation in front of him like a blind man.

Suddenly there was a crash and the sound of a thousand pencils breaking, followed by Calamansi swearing. "Found it," his voice called out somewhere to my left, and I followed. We continued this way for quite some time, I following his voice like the Pied Piper: "Turn left here," "Okay, this way," "Down the slope now" as the suck and hiss of the ocean slowly grew louder. We pushed through the last of the bushes and emerged on the beach, where the first tendrils of orange sunlight began to bloom out over the horizon.

Calamansi pointed to a pile of black volcanic boulders and without saying a word, headed over to it. I followed him, slipping and stumbling up the wet rocks, while he banged shins, elbows, and guitar case up to the highest promontory. "Give me the blanket," he said once I reached the top. He spread out the blanket and we both sat there for a while catching our breath and watching blue spread out over the night-green sea as the sun awakened over the ocean.

"Where are we?" I asked.

Calamansi lay down his guitar case, opened it up, and took out the twelve string. "If I were an educated man or even a smart man," he said as he fine-tuned his guitar, "I would have something good and wise to say to you right now… some kind of speech." I waited while he strummed a chord progression. "Instead, I brought you here to help me greet the sun."

I tried to think what he could mean. "What for?"

"To thank it for the new day." He started playing a slow intro to a song that I had heard all my life but never bothered to listen to. "For being alive."

So I listened. He played and sometimes he sang and sometimes he didn't. And at some point that morning, when all of it became one—his voice, the warmth of my skin, the foaming whitecaps, the whispering low tide, and the music—like a great theatrical background upon which the events of that summer played out like some great prelude, I was there with him, feeling this moment, as real to me as a flat pebble on my tongue. I explored its smooth surface, felt its slippery edges, and sucked in its radiant heat, before opening my eyes and feeling it all slip away, leaving only Calamansi, me, and the emptiness that I could finally acknowledge.

US GUYS AND THE DEVIL

It was the air-conditioning that won us over. While our parents were fuming over the unsuccessful petitions and plotting the political demise of the Devil, he was sagely spending his time giving us rides after school in his air-conditioned Cadillac that was colder on the inside than any of us could imagine.

It started with a contest that someone had come up with: Whoever could keep their hand on the car the longest became the *kodomo taishō* that day, the kid general. It was a brilliant idea because it did not involve athletic ability (which favored the boys) or anything we were supposed to remember from school (which favored the girls); the winner was merely the person who could endure the most pain. Since most of us were just one generation away from immigrant stock, we all felt our pain thresholds had been sufficiently tested despite our tender age.

Everyone knew that the car belonged to the Devil: Who else in Hawaii would own a black car with a black interior? From the time he arrived shortly after sunup, that car baked in the sun at the housing project he was developing next to our lane, so that by the time we got home from school, the car was hotter than lava. This went on for a couple of days: us guys leaving the lane, sneaking over to the building site and laying our hands on the car for the five or ten seconds it would take to determine a winner. We were always careful to make sure that the car was between us and the line of sight of the workers. What we neglected to check was that the car was unoccupied. So, one afternoon right after we had all slapped our hands down onto the car, the passenger door flew open and out stepped the Devil.

Most of us fled like cockroaches caught in the kitchen except Shane, who had his eyes closed. There are two types of kids: those who want to see what is coming at them no matter how painful, and those who can't bear to watch. Shane was one of the latter kind. He closed his eyes during dodgeball, he closed his eyes when we jumped out of the swings, he even closed his eyes when the teacher asked him to spell a word during class. Of course, he would close his eyes when he was enduring the pain of laying hands on the car, and of course he would be the one who got caught.

Shane told us later that what made him open his eyes was not the sound of the car door opening—"I never hear nothing"—but the cool gust that washed over his feet—"Like when the top of the shave ice fall off and you try catch 'em with your feet." The braver among us peeked from wherever we were hiding to see Shane and the Devil conversing, but we couldn't hear them. It seemed like they were talking for quite a while when suddenly Shane got into the car.

We panicked again and raced instinctively back down the lane to the Wongs' covered lanai, our safe haven and command center because of the seven Wong grandchildren. The other asset the Wong grandchildren possessed was their leverage with Goong-Goong Wong, who always seemed to have tea pastries or candied fruits he could give us. Understanding the dire situation we faced and knowing that we would need something extra, the Wong grandchildren decided to send up Aimee, the only granddaughter, to see Goong-Goong. She came back down with a bag of almond cookies, our favorite, and we passed them around and started our discussions.

We knew we would have to mount a rescue party. Some of us were in favor of sending only a small delegation of, say, three kids—Joy as spokesperson since she was *haole* and could speak the best, Darren who was Portuguese like Shane and would pretend to be his brother in case we had to beg, and Mark who owned a baseball bat—while others wanted all of us to go *en masse* as a show of force. We were starting to hammer out a compromise, in which a group of the older kids would go with Mark's bat while the smaller kids stayed behind, when we heard, "Ey! You never saved any for me?"

We turned around to see Shane holding the cookie bag above his head, trying to shake crumbs into his mouth. He stuck his whole face into the bag, and then emerged from it seconds later, his face sprouting yellow crumbs.

"What... where..." we began but Shane just shook his head.

"You guys should ride in that car, get real air-conditioning. It's real cold, too. It's like... like..." Shane paused as he searched for the words. "It's like Sears."

We were too stunned to speak. Sears was our families' refuge when Hawaiian air conditioning—open windows and doors—didn't work, and the humidity of the evening trapped the day's hot air inside the house. On some muggy nights, it seemed like half the island was pretending to shop at Sears. To have Sears comfort available everywhere you went was a luxury unimaginable.

"Come," he said, "We go." And for the first and only time, all of us followed General Shane out of Muliwai Lane to the lot where the Devil's black car stood waiting.

The after school, air-conditioned comfort of the Cadillac was ours for a couple of weeks, and we reveled in it. We established trios in a complex rotation that allowed us to ride with different kids in a different location in the car each time, so that no one could hog the passenger seat next to the Devil. For his part, the Devil never said very much during these trips, only offering us his mysterious smile when we piled into the car at the beginning of our trip and again at the end when we said our thank-yous. He spoke only to Joy, the oldest among us and verging on teen-hood, offering her some anise and fennel seeds he kept in his pockets. She always refused—"Nice girls never accept gifts from old men," she told the Devil—and just watched him pulverize the seeds with his teeth into a mortar that he spit out into the ashtray. He seemed a quiet, harmless old man who possessed a slightly chalky odor like floured bread and a preference for out-of-date black suits that made his bloodless white skin blanch even more by comparison. We treated him as we would treat anybody desirous of and yet uncomfortable with the energy and excitement of children: politely, with a slight touch of pity.

Then one day, the black car was gone. Parked in the spot where it used to wait for us was an army of yellow construction vehicles and workers: men, tanned to the color and texture of tree bark, who joked and cursed incessantly with each other while they worked, their loud voices and even louder laughs heard from any-where in the lane. And while we initially missed the Devil and his car, we quickly took to these men.

At around the same time, notices from the City & County started appearing in our mailboxes. Addressed to our parents and signed by the commissioner, the letters spoke in a dense and arcane vernacular about titles, mandated inspections, code violations, and eminent domain. Though the words were not clear, the tone was: because of their initial protest to his development, the Devil now had his eye on our lane.

As we watched the construction workers after school and on into summer va-cation, we got so used to seeing them around that we named our favorites. The saw operator who ripped pieces of wood all day for the others hated to take his ear plugs in and out, so we named him after what he said most often: "Haaah?" Then there was "No Step," the bulldozer driver who was always telling us to get back—"No step here." But our favorite had to be the foreman that they called Mike but we called "Haunas." Haunas had a great fondness for a game he called "Pull my finger" and often amazed us with the extended solos he performed using, as he said, "Nothing but my natural wind instrument and my wife's cooking." Shane aspired to one day attain his level of artistry.

As the framing for the large condo-type units started going up like the looming skeletons of giants, scrap material was dumped in piles at the edge of the property closest to our lane. For us, the piles were veritable goldmines, and we raided them daily as soon as the last workers left. We were soon surveying plots and raiding our fathers' toolboxes for handsaws and hammers.

We decided to build our clubhouses in the weedy area along Nu'uanu Stream, a sort of no-man's land between the Devil and Muliwai Lane and unobservable from both. Using what we had seen every day as a guide, we divided ourselves into gangs: those who were able to pilfer tools became the carpenters, the more artistic among us became painters and decorators, and the rest of us became hod carriers, picking the choicest material from the scrap pile and dragging it into the high weeds. Because there was so much abundance, we could afford to build clubhouses for everyone, and into that long summer, versicolor shacks nestled like Easter eggs among the weeds on the banks of Nu'uanu Stream.

Like any nascent settlement, once our basic needs for shelter had been met, we started competing with our neighbors. Some of us focused on practical problems like more interior light and designed new walls with window cutouts covered with opaque plastic film. Others chose aesthetic issues and carefully groomed paths and cultivated wildflowers around their structure. However, everyone became more suspicious of the others and more interested in keeping new ideas secret, so perimeter defenses such as phony paths and booby traps built with thorny branches appeared between our clubhouses. Much of that late summer was spent discovering, disarming, and daring each other to breach our latest defense innovation while alliances rose and fell overnight.

Meanwhile, the shadows from the condos grew longer and longer, creating premature sunsets and causing our parents to call us in earlier, curbing our playtime. More and more strangers with clipboards appeared in our lane, pacing off our properties, walking on our roofs, poking beneath our houses, testing our water and electricity. When they were finished, all of them officiously handed our parents a paper for their signature, beginning with things like "The City & County has determined that…" or "The C&C has ordinances that prohibit this…" and our parents would let them go on, nodding their heads as if in agreement, waiting for any hesitation in the stranger's monologue that would let them jump in and quietly explain to the code or health or fire inspector the situation between people "like us" and people "like the Devil." After our parents were done there was always a moment of quiet cogitation before the inspector spoke again, repeating exactly what he had said earlier but smiling and winking at us, forgetting to get our signature or entering a nonexistent house number on the form or mandating repairs but setting deadlines that were far into the next century. If something had to be done, the inspectors were shown the Matsushimas' shed, a buckaloose building that barely provided a roof over the Matsushimas' lawn and gardening tools, a worthy proxy and happy recipient of the orange-and-red "Condemned" stickers that adorned it that summer.

It was on one of those truncated playdays that we heard Shane ripping through the lane on his bike, shouting in kid code, "The Sears stay coming! The Sears stay coming!" Our parents watched us quizzically as we bolted from our tables and out our front doors. We gathered at the dead end of the lane where Shane had ditched his bike.

"I knew he'd come back," he said and pointed over the end of Muliwai Lane, past Nu'uanu Stream, up onto the lot where, sure enough, the Devil's black car could be seen touring his property. He drove slowly and carefully, rounding corners we couldn't see, obeying invisible stop signs, following the plans for a community that only he could envision. We could imagine him spitting licorice paste and smiling to himself as he surveyed his half-dressed creations, making mental notes for his architect and builders. We watched him reach the edge of his property, where, instead of turning around and following his path back out, he swung his car toward the no-man's land of Nu'uanu Stream. He drove along the pruned area of the bank until he reached our clubhouse area hidden in the high weeds, where he stopped suddenly.

The car door opened and the Devil stepped out, dressed in black as always. He walked around to the front of his car where he picked up something from the ground. It was Mark's baseball bat, inadvertently forgotten after one of our fierce internecine battles.

"Oh, that's where it went," Mark muttered. The Devil turned the bat over and contemplated it for a second before indifferently flinging it into the weeds where it hit the side of Mark's clubhouse with a crack as loud as a gunshot. Instinctively, all of us scattered, crouching behind nearby shrubs and garden walls.

As we peeked from our hiding places, we saw the Devil standing in silhouette just in front of the high weeds, hands on hips, craning his neck left and right before slowly turning his visage toward us. We did not emerge until the sound of his car had dissipated into the lamentation of the evening's crickets. We silently dispersed, each solitary save the dread that accompanied us, to return to the sinks full of dirty dishes and other evening chores that awaited us.

The next morning we were awakened by the smell of burning chaff, a choking odor we thought we left behind with the cane fires when our families escaped from the sugar plantations. We raced outside to witness the far bank of Nu'uanu Stream ablaze in an advancing wall of fire, fed by the gasoline the construction workers shook over our clubhouses, leaving in its wake only singed black squares as evidence of a conquered settlement.

We raced out of the lane, a barefoot tribe of pajama-clad homunculi, waving our arms and aiming straight across the building site to the foreman who was busy directing No Step to get more gasoline from the bulldozer.

"Mike! Mike!" we called, resisting the urge to use his Haunas nickname on official business. "Try wait! Try wait!"

Mike nodded for No Step to continue before turning to us. "I'm sorry," he said, "but I had to."

Some of us grabbed his hand while the others pushed him from behind as we literally dragged him into one of the last clubhouses still standing. It belonged to Joy, our best decorator.

"Notice," she said, "what you are standing on." While most of us had been content with dirt floors, Joy had managed to find an array of carpet pieces that she had fanned out in a rainbow, a theme that she pointed out carried over into the painting of the walls, the ceiling, and even the exterior. By this time No Step had arrived with his can of gasoline, so someone ushered him inside.

"Hey look, get cabinets," he pointed out to Mike, and they admired the work of our carpenters and the row of small plywood cabinets with hinges made from squares of roofing paper.

The tour continued on to the outside, where we pointed out the delicate slope of the roof, "'cause sometimes rain plenty and the water got to go somewhere," the latex we coaxed out of the discarded caulking tubes that we used to fill the seams in the wall to keep the insects out "'cause in Hawaii get plenty ants," and we even told them how we had organized ourselves in groups based on their work groups, "'cause you guys da best."

Mike paused and considered something at his feet before lifting his head and smiling. "Well, what can I do," he said to us. He and Mike then shepherded us back from the area, and we all watched silently as the wall of flames jumped ahead and leaped onto the roof of Joy's clubhouse, igniting its rainbow walls, turning them into black peelings that fell off like sunburned skin.

"I'm sorry, but the developer said his insurance doesn't cover unsafe structures on his land," Mike explained to us. "We had to raze them."

We turned to go, the acrid taste of defeat still bitter on our palates, and slouched homeward with war smoldering in our hearts.

The only things we had going into this war—small size, small numbers, and speed—seemed like disadvantages to us until Shane said, "It doesn't take too many mosquitoes to spoil a party," which we adopted as our motto. We moved our command center from the Wongs' lanai to the porch of Mark and Joy's house, which had an unobstructed view of the Devil's lot and his condos. After a few days of observation, we learned that no matter what time the workers arrived in the morning, by three-thirty they were all gone. We created an armory out of a beige '72 Volkswagen Beetle that had been abandoned on our side of Nu'uanu Stream and whose doors were so rusted shut that the only way into or out of the vehicle was crawling through the busted-out back window. We stockpiled any implement that might prove useful in war: baseballs, empty beer bottles, spray paint, old golf clubs, bricks, and even Mrs. Gonzalez's old waffle iron, which did not seem to have an immediate purpose but whose heft promised a destructive potential.

We launched our raid a few nights later. Gathering at the armory until all the troops arrived, we waited until the crickets were loud enough to mask the tramping of our feet before arming ourselves and marching across Nu'uanu Stream and up the bank past the ruins of our former clubhouses, following a course as straight as ants to the nearest condo unit. We poured into the building through the unlocked doors and windows and began driving holes into the wallboard with our golf clubs, flattening the exposed copper plumbing with our bricks, and spray painting crude drawings and obscenities on the newly completed hallways. Only Junior-Boy, the pastor's son who would not take the Lord's name in vain, spray painted in a large looping cursive appropriate biblical passages: "What hath God wrought?" and "He smiteth thee" and the inexplicable "The children of this world are in their generation wiser than the children of light."

We duplicated our atrocities upon another building before retreating back across the stream to disarm and race into our houses before our parents missed us for bath and bedtime. We spent a leisurely evening in the soporific waters and took to bed right away, still warm from the glow of our baths and the revenge we sipped and savored like a glass of warm milk.

The next morning we woke bright and early and streamed onto Mark and Joy's porch to see the reaction of the Devil. All day long we waited for that black car to tear into the lot and the Devil to fly out of it, shaking his head and clenching his fists as he inspected the damage, coming out of the buildings and recognizing us, maybe shaking his fist, shouting a threat or two, any reaction that we could imitate and mock for months. But he never showed up. Not that day, not the next, or even the day after that. After three days of watching Haunas and his men take pieces of damaged hallway and copper tubing out of the condos and replace it with new wallboard and plumbing, all we had succeeded in doing was creating more work for the crew and deepening our own sense of impotence.

For days afterward we shuffled through our games of kickball or tag, breaking them early to sit on the curb and mope. Even our parents seemed to get into the spirit, returning home depressed after zoning meetings in which their words of "common sense" and "inappropriate residential densities" were put down by the commissioner's words of "not illegal" and "very important member of the business community." All the while the Devil's bright white slabs rose above our street like a row of perfect teeth. We might have been stuck like that for weeks if someone hadn't said, "Boy, I like do to him what he did to us," to which Junior-Boy replied, "Yeah, an eye for an eye," to which PP asked after a long pause, "Isn't there a can of gas for the lawnmower in the Matsushimas' shed?"

Newly revived, we sprang into action, assigning Shane to filch the matches from his father, who, despite being unemployed for as long as any of us could remember, never seemed to be in short supply of cigarettes, matches, and beer. Since it was his idea, PP volunteered to retrieve the gasoline from the shed, and the rest of us climbed up Joy and Mark's porch once again to scout out which of the Devil's buildings we would burn down as he did ours. At first, we chose one of the tall slabs in the middle, creating a vacancy in the perfect hegemony, like a boxer's gap-toothed grin, but we realized that a fire that large would be uncontrollable. Instead, we picked a small two-story building still in its infancy, naked and vulnerable in its plywood exterior.

PP, or Pyro Paul, was our most experienced firebug. He had gained his knowledge from a lifelong passion of the pyrotechnic arts, starting with magnifying glasses and melted army men and graduating to tending the yard waste fires of the lane. He reasoned this would be a "quick operation, a two-man job at most" and tapped his younger brother Mini-P as his partner. His plan was simple: They would trot up to the building with their gasoline and matches after dark, Mini-P would wait outside as a lookout while PP doused the interior with gasoline, and just after exiting the building, PP would throw the lighted matchbook inside and give the can to Mini-P, "because in case we get caught, the person who lit the fire shouldn't be carrying a can of gas." PP would leave by means of the street, whereas Mini-P would return to the lane through Nu'uanu Stream with the gas can.

The rest of us agreed our best course of action would be to not endanger the operation and to carry on with our nightly routines, so later that night as we ate dinner with our families, fought with our brothers and sisters for the bathroom, and finally went to bed, we resisted the temptation to sneak outside and see the two brothers standing in silhouette against their flaming orange and red background.

The next morning we waited until all the fire engines had left and most of the smoke had lifted before we scrambled onto Mark and Joy's porch to survey the brothers' handiwork. We were greeted by the sight we had hoped for: the Devil's black Caddy idling outside of his half-consumed building. The building hadn't burned to the ground as we had expected, but through the vacant eyes of the windowless structure, we could see that most everything on the inside had burned off, leaving only scorched black walls on the outside. We were clapping the brothers on the back and celebrating PP's arsonous talents when we noticed the Devil exiting his burned building. He conferred a few seconds with Haunas, and then without even looking at us, climbed into his car and drove away.

"Lookit," Mini-P said, breaking our silence. "He's running scared."

And with that pronouncement, we all celebrated some more. Some of us ran off to bring back juice and cookies, some of us returned with our water guns and water balloons, and Joy brought out her phonograph with her ABBA records. It was our own private street fair, where we invented games and dance moves and reveled in the youthful exuberance that none of us would ever feel again. Only later that afternoon, full from sugared snacks and liquids, soaking wet, and tired from dancing and ducking water gunfire, did we notice that the workers had spent their day constructing a chain link fence around the building we had burned.

We were dumbfounded. Joy turned off the phonograph and we all stared at what seemed like the stupidest move in the world.

"He thinks we have a grudge against that one building," Junior-Boy said.

"We should burn down the rest of the condos," PP said.

"Oh, what's the point?" Joy said. "He would just think we were mad at those buildings as well."

Gloom sank over us again as we learned that our nemesis, far from the wily plotter and mastermind that our parents said he was, was actually an idiot. And we knew from our experiences in dealing with hardheaded teachers and unjust vice-principals that trying to communicate with an idiot was ultimately a fruitless act.

The rest of that summer flagged off into a passive ennui as we watched Haunas and the crew restore the building we had tried to destroy and then put the finishing facades on the rest of the property. Truckloads of sod carried the putting-green lawns that sprung up overnight, wandering hibiscus and bougainvillea were replaced with tourist flowers that incessantly bloomed for two weeks and had to be replaced, and crews with snarling chainsaws leveled almost all of the trees on the property, exposing Nu'uanu Stream and its community of crawfish and sunfish to a harsh sunlight that killed off in weeks what had taken millennia to develop.

Even our parents' talk turned from resistance to resignation, as first one neighbor and then another suddenly became quiet and inactive. They began selling their land for reasons we could not blame them for: the inspector who found the Nakahara house termite ridden; the stroke that left Grandpa Ka'ai suddenly confined to his bed after forty years of walking a beat in Chinatown, giving his children no choice but to move him into a convalescent home; and the enforcement of a residential zoning regulation which forced Widow Gonzalez to close her take-in dressmaking and alterations business and abandon her only means of income.

In those final weeks before school started, we could feel the end coming. The signs were all around us: the strained conversations and short tempers of our parents; the lane unraveling at the edges as properties were sold and suddenly placed off-limits; and the coming of the new school year bringing an end to our furlough of summer freedom. We watched as the people trickling into the Model Condo & Sales Office grew into an unstoppable stream on the weekends, the lines forming early and pushing out to the sidewalk where the Devil had planted the hand-carved, gilded herald for his community, "Lone Pine," in front of the only tree he had left untouched on the original property, a lonely fifty-foot pine.

A pine held very little meaning for us: you couldn't steal fruit from it like a mango, it didn't have windfall blossoms to make *lei* with like a plumeria, it didn't even attract the enormous roaches that favored the banana. Perhaps if the Devil hadn't named the property as he had, we would not have noticed the tree. But here, after the Devil had denuded the property except for one remnant of the past, and then framed and displayed it in a splendid isolation, did we notice a tree that seemed to be yet another agent in obedience to the Devil.

Unlike our other undertakings that summer, we did not even discuss this one. Whoever was the first person to gather up dry brush and pile it under the lone pine we have never known, never needed to know, because on that Sunday evening in late August, hours after the Lone Pine Model Condo & Sales Office had closed, we were all ferrying dead weeds and other detritus up the hill from our side of Nu'uanu Stream to the pyre under the lone pine.

We worked silently, almost reverently, forming a ring of combustibles around the base of the pine till it was knee-deep. We looked at PP, who motioned us back before he jogged a couple of revolutions around the tree, flicking lit matches into the pyre with a hiss. Flickers of flame rose unsteadily from new birth and then bloomed into flaming tulips that partnered with others as they danced across the pyre. Gray smoke surged out of the pile as the flames, now a single pulsating body, jumped onto the pine's lowest branches where it raced up the tree in no time, transforming it into a giant torch alight from top to bottom.

Enveloped in flames, the tree roared like a live thing and we stood transfixed, reading in the glow of the flames all of the events of that summer and our part in each of them. Out of that roiling stink of burning pine, Joy said, "We look like Halloween," and we looked at each other illuminated by the firelight and could finally see that in the end, it was not anger but fear that the Devil had impressed upon the faces of all of us.

Suddenly, there was a tremendous crack, followed by a rain of small flames and burning debris as branches started cascading down. We pulled PP away from there and ran home because we knew there was nothing else we could do.

In a little less than a week, the Devil had replaced the charred trunk and its fancy sign with a generic metal sign, painted all white and announcing a new name, "Far Acres," in black block letters. For a while, our parents had fun with this new name, using it as an example of the Devil's idiocy, because who in Hawaii can afford to talk about acres when you live on an island. But by the next summer, the Devil would have successfully consumed all of Muliwai Lane, our houses flattened to pave a massive driveway. This driveway allowed the sanitation trucks to access the gigantic garage that housed the rolloff waste containers that were needed to support his development, leaving only the stink of rotting rubbish and the view of the garbage garage's imposing backside as compensation for our broken community.

WOOING ELIZABETH

When people asked my Aunt Elizabeth about Uncle Mike, she would tell them, "Oh, he's at HCC," hoping they would think he was teaching classes or something at Honolulu Community College, when in reality, anyone who knew anything about him would know she really meant the Halawa Correctional Center. He was serving a four-year sentence in minimum security for fraud—"simple fraud," he would remind me every visit—for impersonating a *nakahodo*, or traditional Japanese matchmaker, who had died ten years earlier on an outer island. Uncle Mike had been really good at handicapping grooms, brides, families, and occupations the way he used to handicap jockeys, horses, trainers, and track conditions. By transforming his extensive bookmaking knowledge with its probabilities and percentages and leveraging the reputation of the real *nakahodo*, he had created a clientele and a growing reputation for himself on Oahu. Up until the day he was arrested, he would say he owed all of his success to Elizabeth, the woman who had "taught him the bonds of true love."

Aunt Elizabeth was my real aunt, deeded by blood and my mother's only sister, whereas Uncle Mike had only married in. However, not unlike the sympathy engendered between wary neighbors when faced by a common enemy, I always felt close to the men who became our uncles by marriage to Elizabeth. I could not imagine marriage with Aunt Elizabeth, the most grown-up person I knew. She was pretty—"pretty like the serpent in the Garden of Eden," as my mother liked to say—and the only woman in our family who wore high heels all of the time. Never once had I seen her in the flats our mothers had retired to long ago. She smoked like a movie star, elegantly and continuously, through long black holders to avoid leaving smears of lipstick on the cigarette, a sight she found vulgar. And like many great personalities, she habitually spoke of herself in the third person, a tendency I discovered at the age of five, when I brought her my favorite board game. She looked down at me, arched her perfectly plucked eyebrow into a talon and said, "No one has explained it to you, have they?"

I shook my head.

"Aunt Elizabeth doesn't do this shit," she said, "She doesn't play Chutes n' Ladders."

She paused to blow smoke in my face. "Do you understand?"

I nodded, "Aunt Elizabeth is no fun."

"Good boy," she said patting my head like a puppy. "Now run along and find that useless uncle of yours so he can get Aunt Elizabeth a drink."

So Uncle Mike and I grew close, drawn by our completely opposite yet similarly intense feelings for Elizabeth, and it seemed natural when he recruited me to be his assistant. Business had really picked up at that point, with Uncle Mike attending anywhere from six to ten weddings a weekend, and when he looked at me, he saw a branch office, an expansion of his matrimonial services. At first, he tried to involve me in every aspect of the business, explaining the arcane ranking system he plugged into the elaborate equations he had developed for producing lasting marriages at a ninety-three percent success rate, the highest of any *nakahodo* in the islands, and far above that of his namesake. But after a few months, it became apparent to both of us that I was not worthy of the profession. "Matchmaking is a matter of patient observation," he would say. Clearly, at fourteen, I was neither patient nor observant enough. The women I judged too ugly he would relabel as kind and point out my oversight: her second toe was longer than her big toe—a sure sign of intelligence. The guys I okayed as husband material he would just groan at and point out they came straight to the interview from a hasty shower with hair still wet, an indication of a hidden family history of mental abnomalities (wet hair = soft head). "You can't rush to judge," he told me once. "It's like picking a melon." By the end, I was involved only in the purely clerical aspects of the business—setting up the client meetings, routing photos to parents and prospectives, updating the rosters of potentials, and keeping his calendar of appointments—areas at which I excelled by keeping careful and comprehensive notes. Notes that turned out to be quite helpful to state prosecutors.

Still, after he was convicted ("not by the clients, did you notice none of them testified for the prosecution?") and sentenced ("even the judge admitted that on balance I had probably produced more happiness in the world than pain") and publicly disavowed by Aunt Elizabeth ("that crack about men being unreliable income hurt worst of all"), Uncle Mike continued to keep up a relationship with me, much to the dismay of the family. For the four years he was locked up, as I moved from freshman to senior in high school, he sent me letters and packages regularly. They were a great embarrassment to my mother and her sister because they smelled like the ashtray of a hotel lobby and were stamped all over in red ink: "NOTE: This correspondence has been sent by an inmate of the Halawa Correctional Center." Mother would burn with shame and apologize to the mailman profusely every time he delivered a package from Uncle Mike, but I suspect the mailman looked forward to these deliveries as much as I did. He would always ask me about them the next day, and I would show him the latest prison handicraft Uncle Mike had created: an American flag made from strips of pornographic magazines with cigarette filter stars, a portrait of Jesus made from cigarette ash and hair from the prison barbershop, iridescent black earrings and matching necklace made from cockroach carapaces, and an evening bag made from the silver foil of used cigarette packs which I was to give to the "girl who had eyes, well, eye for me."

That was his little joke. Sara, the girl, did not even know I existed. But throughout his incarceration he had seen my growing interest in members of the fairer sex and was the only one in my family who seemed genuinely interested in my burgeoning romantic life ("no one longs for romance more than a prisoner"). So I had told him about my attraction to a girl in my class who terrified me with her haughty demeanor and fatal vanity. Most of the other guys in school called it a defect, but as I explained to Uncle Mike, Sara's eye, not the plain right eye but the left one with its languid eyelid, drooped so seductively that she simultaneously wore an expression of schoolgirl innocence and a madame's world-weary disdain. While her regular eye stood as naked as the day she was born, Sara favored the other eyelid with shadow in dramatic hues of blue and green, applied with a heavy hand. She was like no other girl in school, and that eye summoned all my young blood. When residual tremors worked her eyelid into a perpetual coquettish half-wink, it was like a flashing beacon to me, a green light in my age of stumbling adolescence.

For years I admired her from afar, sitting in our English classes, watching her read from the misanthropic admonitions of Frost at the front of the class. As she tilted her head back to expose her alabaster neck, the good eye opened wide like a gun fighter sighting along the barrel, while the other fluttered like a gaudy butterfly wing, as if to wink at everyone in the room at once. I purposefully sabotaged my own math tests and quizzes, just so I could remain in her classes and sit close enough to watch her tackle word problems, the frustration of which sent her lips pouting till they were like a couple of well-fed caterpillars, a sight that stirred my lust-addled imagination and sent my heart racing.

All might have remained this way until the end of my senior year had Uncle Mike not been paroled early for what he would tell everyone was "good behavior"—a term defined by the authorities to mean, as he confided to me on our drive home from HCC, that he had been released in return for scuttling his jailhouse lawsuit suing the state for prison overcrowding.

"You see," he told me as we pulled into the driveway of my mom's house, where she had taken in Aunt Elizabeth, "everything in life can be negotiated as long as both parties can be convinced that they are really both headed in the same direction."

"Like the early release of a troublemaker," I said, killing the car.

"Like love," he said as he watched Aunt Elizabeth lean over the railing of the porch to peer into the car. We watched her face go from slack to horror before it finally hardened into disgust. She skipped over Uncle Mike to shake her head pointedly at me while mouthing a profanity before throwing up her hands and marching back into the house.

It took me three days of pleading before they let him stay. All my arguments about Uncle Mike—this man, one of the most celebrated unionists of our time, the likes of which we may never see again, the man whom couples all over this island were still giving prayers of thanks to, yes, this great man had literally no place to live—fell on the deaf ears and dead coral hearts of my mother and Elizabeth.

"Ugh, that man," Aunt Elizabeth said in a voice loud enough to be heard by the neighbors and Uncle Mike, who sat in my car waiting out my negotiations. "He's like a warm pile of something I stepped in and need to scrape from the bottom of my shoe."

On day two, I turned to logic, arguing that with Dad long dead and I just a mere lad of seventeen, we had a perfect and temporary substitute for the man about the house.

"Yes, we do," my mother said sweetly, "that's what Elizabeth is for."

On day three, when they saw I was going to follow through on my threat to let Uncle Mike live in my Volkswagen and had brought home a plastic wading pool and a gentle sprinkler head to rig up as a bathtub, they relented.

"If I must be humiliated," Aunt Elizabeth said to me, with a glare so fierce she could stare down Medusa, "at least keep him tied up in the backyard where the neighbors won't see him."

And so, Uncle Mike moved into the garden shed and out of my car so I could air out the interior from three days of cigarette smoke and unwashed funk. After I told him what Aunt Elizabeth said—"the man has been in prison, you think he can live without rules?"—I laid down the terms she dictated: He must remain fully clothed at all times ("Ahh, she remembers how uncomfortable pants used to make me"); he was not allowed to come out of the shed until Aunt Elizabeth has left for work ("That's okay, she has a tendency to talk too much in the morning, anyway"); he was not allowed in the house at any time for any reason and must go to the YMCA to take care of his "personal habits" ("Only your aunt would call going to the bathroom a 'habit'"); and he could only return to the shed after dark. This last one gave him pause.

"Like an illicit lover," he said finally.

I shook my head. "C'mon, I'll help you move some of this junk."

While I arranged bags of grass seed and fertilizer to fashion him a bed, Uncle Mike explained to me how he had spent many nights in prison thinking about the similarities between my situation with Sara and his with Elizabeth.

"You see, a woman's heart is like a still, quiet pond in a lonely meadow. And you and me, we men, are like dragonflies beating our wings above that pond," he explained, flapping his arms for illustration. "Only when we beat our wings longly and strongly enough will the ripples of love appear on the surface of that pond."

Uncle Mike leaned back and sucked on his cigarette. I waited for more but since nothing was coming, I just nodded to myself for a time and acted as if I understood what he had just uttered.

"Does that mean you're going back to matchmaking?"

He shook his head. "A condition of my parole."

I nodded.

"Not for anyone else, anyway," he added.

"She told me when it came up to say, 'Not a chance in hell.'"

Uncle Mike just chuckled.

But Aunt Elizabeth, she was taking no chances. That first Saturday after Uncle Mike moved in, she informed me that I was to cancel any plans I had that day and drive her way out on the North Shore side to pick up some boxes. When I protested the late notice and total disregard for my social life, she said, "Since when have you had a social life?" When I retorted something about my private life, she just snorted and laughed so hard she had to put down her cigarette. I waited for her to catch her breath.

"I wouldn't call those titty magazines under your bed a private social life," she managed to say before breaking into another round of laughter. She wiped her eyes with one hand and with the other jerked her thumb over her shoulder in the direction of the backyard. "Besides, you owe me for letting you keep that stray."

I put on my coat and stalked off to the car.

Of course, neither of us had been that far in the country before, and so I spent the entire morning driving around the unmarked streets of the North Shore while Aunt Elizabeth repeated over and over, "There's only one goddamn main road out here, how can we be lost?" I knew enough about Aunt Elizabeth to not answer the question, unlike the helpless gas station employees we left in our wake whose ears are probably still ringing from the abuse she heaped upon them and their "idiotic and illiterate" landmark directions ("you'll go past six yellow poles on the left, and then turn right before the chain-link fence...") Even now, I'm sure there are at least a few people on the North Shore whose nightmares begin with a pair of determined high-heeled shoes stepping out of a beige Volkswagen Beetle.

It wasn't until early evening when we eventually found the place, Queen's Ranch, more by having been everywhere else than by accurate directions. Aunt Elizabeth pointed me toward a dirt path that led to a small house. As we drove down the path, I still expressed my doubts about the place because I had not seen a sign or marker.

"No, I'm sure of it," she said as she pointed out the window. "The owners said something about a yard full of boxes."

On both sides of the driveway stood stands of white wooden boxes, stacked waist high and arranged in rows as orderly as a cemetery. We filed past these silent sentries till we reached the house, where I was instructed to wait in the car until she called for me. I watched Aunt Elizabeth march onto the porch and look down to smooth out her skirt, before knocking on the door. I was too far away to hear their conversation, but she started talking as soon as the door opened, and they must have been going at it awhile because the next thing I knew, I was jolted awake by Aunt Elizabeth pounding on the windshield.

"Why in the Christ's sake do you have your keys in your ear," she asked. "No wonder you couldn't hear me!"

I reached up and pulled the keys out of my ear. One of the first things Uncle Mike had shown me was how he learned to clean his ears in prison. The secret to cleaning your ears with a key, he said, was using the flat top part of the key, not the jagged bottom part, to scrap around in there. With enough practice, it was possible to channel the wax into the grooves of the key, which was how the inmates competed with each other. Quantity was king, and Uncle Mike had won many a cigarette by being able to pack the grooves on both sides of a key. At first I tried it out of curiosity but once I got the hang of it, cleaning my ear this way produced a soothing soporific effect on me, almost like hypnosis, which coupled with daydreams of Sara must have lulled me to sleep, mid-swab. "I was…" I said as I stumbled out of the car, "That is, Uncle Mike taught me…"

"Ugh, some disgusting habit, I'm sure. I do not want to hear it." She pointed to a stack of white boxes on the end of the porch. "Just go pick those up and put them into the car."

As anyone who has ever owned a Beetle remembers, the roomiest spot in the car is the passenger seat, where anything big, bulky, or in my case, boxy, had to sit. Even if something could fit in the backseat, it had to get past the bottleneck of the folded-down front seats, an acrobatic struggle usually not worth the effort. I managed to wedge one box at the foot of the passenger seat and stack the remaining three onto the seat, where they would stay if held them up with my shoulder and my head as I drove. That left Aunt Elizabeth clutching two small plastic boxes, standing outside the vehicle shaking her head at me.

"Of course, you couldn't buy a car where you could tie something on the roof," she said.

I shrugged and waited for her to take off her high heels before helpfully shoving her into the back seat. As we drove away with my head pressed up against the stacked boxes like a lover, I could hear Aunt Elizabeth's discontented mumbling grow into an angry hum in the backseat.

Once we got back home, Aunt Elizabeth immediately ordered me to stack two of the boxes in the backyard near one side of the house and stack the other two in the back on the other side of the house while she "finds some way to escape from this ridiculous backseat with some dignity." I took my time about it, picking the spots deliberately, tamping down the area with my shoes so that it would be level, and then carefully stacking the boxes with exaggerated precision, hoping that by concentrating, I could silence the reverberations echoing in my brain from the drive where my head struck like a clapper on the side of the wooden box at every road imperfection.

"Get out of the way," Aunt Elizabeth said as I was making minute adjustments to the stack. "I'm putting her in."

I stepped back as Aunt Elizabeth slid the top of the box off and placed the smaller box inside. She fiddled for a couple of seconds inside the box before quickly sliding the top back on. "Again," she said and I followed her to the other side of the yard where she repeated her movements on that stack of boxes. After sliding that top back on, she turned and paused just long enough to side-eye the shed (where Uncle Mike was presumably watching all of this) before saying, "Follow me."

I trotted out of the backyard following her like an obedient manservant, around to the front to the porch, where she slapped a thick leather-bound book onto my chest and slipped a $20 into my palm before rolling my fingers into it and crushing my hand for emphasis.

"Every week you keep them alive, you'll get another $20."

She turned and entered the house before I looked down at the book. The gold embossing on the cover winked at me as I read its title: *The ABC of Bee Culture*.

For twenty dollars a week, I did surprisingly little. Sure, I worried about our couple hundred new boarders for the first two weeks, coming home after school and pouring a solution of two parts sugar and one part water over the comb frames every other day, but after they started building new combs, I closed the hive cover and left them alone. Since I knew that Aunt Elizabeth detested pets ("if I needed someone to sit next to me on the couch and leave its hair all over the floor, I'd just find another man"), I figured that she was going to put the bees to work like she did everybody else. But she seemed indifferent to the idea of a late summer harvest of honey, and I knew I could really stop studying the "Honey Extraction" section when I finally learned the real reason for keeping the bees.

"Yep, I'm allergic to bees," Uncle Mike said merrily. "Like a death sentence with my allergies."

One sting, he claimed, was all it would take, but the possibility seemed to make him giddy, something I could not understand.

"No wonder you've not gotten anywhere with Sara," he said. "Women like Sara and Elizabeth court love, and love is a coy mistress."

"Coy mistress?" Aunt Elizabeth was the poster child of the uncoy. If coy was a delicate flower growing between the cracks of a sidewalk, then Aunt Elizabeth was the speed demon that jumps the curb to barrel over it.

"Sure," he maintained. "She really wants me to approach her, charm her again, like the old days. But she is going to make it as hard as humanly possible for me to do it."

"And that's a good thing?"

"Sure, it shows she cares."

"Or that she hates you."

"No, if she really hated me, would she have put me out here where she can see me every night while she is washing dishes?" Uncle Mike then turned toward the kitchen window and smiled while nodding his head. I looked just in time to see Aunt Elizabeth roll her eyes and close the curtains, before yelling something to my mother about buying a shade for the window.

"It's second nature to women," he whispered confidentially, "to be really good at exploiting men's weaknesses."

I thought about that for a moment. "You mean like when Sara is chewing gum, and she looks over at me and that gum and her eye seem to be working in tandem, and at the very apogee of that motion, she creates a kind of smirk, a knowing snarl, almost, that seems to know the racing of my heartbeat and everything I am feeling at that moment?"

Uncle Mike was silent and looked at me quizzically for a long time. "Sure, like that. I guess."

I just nodded and we both leaned against the shed and ruminated on our private fantasies for a long time.

There was one thing Uncle Mike knew he needed to prove before Aunt Elizabeth would take him back. He knew he had to become "reliable income." Luckily, in prison he had a lot of time to think about it, and in minimum security, there were many well-educated, white-collar criminals to give him advice. He had come out of prison with a philosophy: that identity cons, like the one he perpetrated, were limited because he was basically selling his time, which meant that he could only make money when he was in front of the mark. And while not really remorseful ("because really, all I did was make people's dreams come true"), he did understand that he took advantage of people like himself, local people trying to get by. What he needed to do was turn his attention to the endless spring of opportunity that flowed into Hawaii by the minute: the tourists. So he imported bags of paste shells from the Philippines, strung them together on a *lei*, spray painted them in whatever colors were on sale at the hardware store, and spent his days going door-to-door in Waikīkī convincing store owners to carry his rare *lei* made from the discarded shells of nearly extinct land snails who lived only on the steepest pali cliffs of Hawaii.

"By creating objects of fraud that can be sold at any time," he told me, "you can make money even when you are sleeping."

He was an instant success. His labor costs (me) were cheap, his overhead (the shed) was free, and he could take most of the markup when he sold to the middlemen, just like he had planned it in "P-school," as he called his business school education. And I? I was getting rich. By collecting twenty dollars a week for doing basically nothing for Aunt Elizabeth and getting twenty-five cents apiece for finished *lei*, I was topping out at almost $200 a week with no time to spend it.

So it came as a surprise one Thursday after school when, after months of emptying shoeboxes of baseball cards and filling them with cash, our weekly delivery from the Philippines didn't arrive. It was my job to open the hundred-pound bags of fake shells where they dumped them in the driveway and transport them, bucket by bucket, to the cleaning station (garden hose) before emptying the shells onto the drying rack (picnic table). When I ran to tell Uncle Mike the news, I found him sitting in the yard in the shade of his shed, his back leaning against the wall. He acknowledged that the delivery had not come, and in fact would never come again, because he had decided to call it quits.

"Why?"

"Women like men who take chances," Uncle Mike said by way of explanation.

"What?"

"Women like men who take chances," he repeated. Then when he saw I wasn't getting it, he sighed and shook his head. "Look at your aunt over there."

I looked over to where he pointed and saw Aunt Elizabeth watering the flowers in her backyard garden. Ever since the bees had arrived, she had taken a renewed interest in her garden and was unusually gentle watering the flowers to avoid the flower centers and inadvertently wetting a bee.

"Do you know why she is happy?" he asked.

I suddenly imagined Uncle Mike grabbing his neck and hitting the ground as if he had been shot and Aunt Elizabeth rising behind him, holding a straw and a fistful of bees. "Yes, I think so..."

"She's happy because I have no place in the world," he said. "Women need a man they can look up to, because sometimes in the end, that's all both of them can hold onto, his place in the world." He paused to yank out some blades of grass that seemed to offend him. "And what am I? I make trinkets. A shell peddler. Who would look up to that?"

I shrugged my shoulders and turned my attention to Aunt Elizabeth. She put the hose down to flood her garden and seemed to be talking to the bees as they wandered from flower to flower. "My precious darlings," I thought I heard her say, so I stepped closer and heard her say it again before I believed it. Although I was her favorite among all the nephews and nieces, she had never uttered a single endearment to me unless you count the time she had called me "Old Shit-for-brains" after I tried to disprove the comedy routine of slipping on a banana peel. I had raced my bike toward a pile of banana peels and stopped suddenly after hitting the first ones, which not only caused my bike to slip out from under me but lubricated the skid that sent me careening into a neighbor's stone wall, where I hit so hard I lost some teeth, got two black eyes, and ended up with an oozing scrape on the side of my face the shape of California. Aunt Elizabeth was the first adult on the scene and, as always, the first with an unforgettable comment. Since most of us were too young to swear openly at that time, all the kids abbreviated and called me "Old SFB" that entire summer.

"C'mon, admit it, don't you miss the old glamour and excitement? Working with real people, real emotions?" he asked.

"I'd rather not have to go to court again," I said.

"Then help me out with something," he said. "A business opportunity."

"What is it?"

"I can't say yet," he said, standing up. "But having changed marriage in these islands, I want to move on to a greater challenge."

"Greater challenge?"

"I can't do it without you," he said.

I thought about it. It sounded bad. Getting people married was one thing, you could always erase that by getting a divorce. But something greater sounded ominous. Irreversible. People hardly had a sense of humor about what was supposed to be the happiest day of their life. And they still threw Uncle Mike in jail for it. I couldn't imagine something greater that wouldn't end up with me in jail as well. All my good sense was telling me no. No way. Out of the question. Old Shit-for-brains had learned his lesson. "Okay."

"Good," he said, clapping me on the back. "Now, I'll need a couple of those shoeboxes."

"Okay."

"And I'll need you to sell your car."

"What?"

Two days later, in the middle of Sawada's math class, during a test that was supposed to challenge our understanding of sine, cosine, and tangent as it applied to the construction of a problematic bridge, in which I had spent most of my time watching Sara nibble vexedly on the eraser of her pencil, horrified by the fact that as the eraser disappeared, she appeared to spit none of it out and was, in fact, literally eating her pencil, while simultaneously fighting my arousal over a fantasy I had created in which she was a vampiress and I, a willing victim, Uncle Mike showed up at the classroom door. Of course, he couldn't just discreetly slip into the class and ask the teacher for permission to see me like anybody else would have done. No, he stood in the doorway and shouted at Miss Sawada, "Hey, I know you. Didn't I marry off your sister, several years ago?"

Everyone stopped and turned toward the door. Except me. I just closed my eyes.

"Yes," said Sawada, "That was my cousin."

"I remember you from the wedding party," Uncle Mike said. I could imagine him with a big grin across his face, surveying the classroom. "I remember looking at the wedding party and thinking, 'I would have had an easier time pairing up you, the pretty one.'"

The class erupted into laughter. I just groaned. It was his standard line when he was in the business: No matter how ugly, or in this case, old and crotchety the person was, he would say "the pretty one."

"Anyway, I'm here for my nephew," he said. "Says he sits next to the prettiest girl in school…"

Suddenly all eyes were on me and in my panic, I stood and made the mistake of taking a quick glance at Sara. All eyes then turned to her, and they all saw what I did, her one unfettered eye wide in wonder and surprise, while the special one, my beloved one, trembled in a palsy of outrage and disgust. I rushed toward Uncle Mike, hitting him square in the chest like a lineman and pushing him out the door, but not before he was able to point and say, "Is that her?"

Laughter followed me out of the classroom. I pushed him backwards all the way down the hall as he just laughed and told me to calm down. I stopped when we got all the way to the stairwell, and only because he owed me four shoeboxes full of money.

"Listen, she will love you soon enough."

"Not with that stunt," I fumed. "What do you want?"

"I need the car. I found a buyer."

"In two days?"

"Yeah, I know this guy, actually, I don't really know him but he's the cousin of the *hanai* brother of the guy in the cell across from mine…"

"Okay, okay, never mind," I said, turning to go back to the classroom. "Take the car."

"No worry," Uncle Mike said to my back. "You needed a warning shot. Guarantee she cannot help but notice you now."

When I got back to class I went straight back to my seat, but everyone continued to sit there and look at me with stupid grins and expectant looks on their faces. It was as if I had just arrived with the punch line of a joke they had been waiting for all day, and I knew life would not return to normal until I served up a suitable ending to this anecdote that would be all over school before lunchtime.

"He needed the car, my car," I explained to Miss Sawada, loud enough for the whole class to hear. I heard a few people chuckle, and by the time I returned to my seat, most everyone was back at their tests. Everyone, that is, but Sara, who was staring at her paper though I could tell she was not really concentrating because she had not resumed eating her pencil. The whole thing made me sigh, and just when I started reading the first problem, I heard a "Psst! Psst!"

Everyone looked up, and there was Uncle Mike at the door acting out an elaborate pantomime of trying to start a car, but horrors! He has no key! He searched his pockets and patted himself down in an elaborate parody of guard searches in prison, except he lovingly lingered near his crotch, feeling himself down with a kind of hip-swiveling action that got some of the girls in class giggling.

"Hey, brah," some joker said. "He need the car key!"

I stood up, reached into my pocket and threw the car keys as hard as I could at Uncle Mike. He caught them without a problem and then pantomimed an elaborate thank-you before slipping out of the doorway. The room was silent for a moment before someone said, "What, he no like borrow your shoes, too?"

And while everyone was laughing, I sneaked a peek at Sara, who was laughing also, and for the first time, had both eyes on me, unblinking.

When I got home from school that day, a black hearse was parked on the lane in front of the house. The car was so long it blocked the width of the entire front yard, and I marveled at the tinted windows and gawked at the polished silver adornments on the sides until I suddenly remembered Uncle Mike's allergy and our lethal little neighbors. With fear sinking like a rock in my gut, I raced around the house to the backyard, but instead of seeing a crowd of medical and police officials standing around the prone body of Uncle Mike, I saw him standing alone with his back to me in one corner of the yard, relieving himself.

"Just watering the grass," he explained as he zipped himself up.

"The car... I thought..."

"You like it?" he said, as he put his arm over my shoulder and guided me around to the side of the house. "I traded that Volkswagen for it."

"You what?"

"You're right," he admitted. "I wish I had gotten a deal that good. I had to give him some cash, too."

By that time we had arrived in the front and were standing directly in front of the vehicle. "You bought a hearse?"

"It's our company car."

"An old hearse?"

"It's a Cadillac," he said as he walked beside it, petting it in measured strokes as if he were sizing up a racehorse. "A Brougham Special Limousine."

"It's a hearse! You traded in my car for a hearse!"

"Now calm down," he said. He brought his hand to his face and started stroking his chin. He did it when he was surprised or nervous. It was his only tell. "I did say this was our company car, didn't I? Which means it is half yours…"

"Half a hearse? What am I going to do, drive this thing to school?" I couldn't even imagine the ridicule I would receive from every social strata in high school when I pulled into the school lot. And all of it, all of it, would be deserved.

"No, not to school, because I need to use it during the day," he said. "But you could use it on dates with that eye girl or going to the football games or something."

I just shook my head and sat down. I buried my face in my hands. "I'm going to date Sara in a hearse."

"Really, it's a kind of limousine."

I looked up at him. "Yeah, a limousine for dead people!"

He nodded and sat down next to me. "But not anymore. We're not going to be carting around dead people."

"We're not?"

He shook his head. "Promise."

"Then what did you…"

"…we…"

"Then what did WE buy a hearse… I mean limousine for?"

Uncle Mike smiled at my little slip. "You see, that's the way to get with the program."

Mom waited till Aunt Elizabeth got home before she took her out onto the porch and gave her my explanation: that I now owned a hearse with Uncle Mike and that we were going to park in front of the house like this since it was too long and much too wide to go into the carport, and frankly, I didn't see a problem because other families had to park on the lane as well. There was a moment of silence before Aunt Elizabeth roared out my name. I slunk out to the porch.

"You don't think there is a problem parking a hearse in front of the house," Aunt Elizabeth said in the kind of calm that never failed to remind me of the phrase "the calm before the shit hits the fan."

"Limousine," I corrected. "Limousine."

Aunt Elizabeth looked at me for a long time, then looked at my mother, who shrugged. "It's a hearse."

"It's a Cadillac," I tried. "A Cadillac Special something something Limousine."

"Okay, deaf ear," she said. "You don't think there is a problem parking a damn something something limousine, a former meat wagon for the make-die-dead, in front of our house?"

She waited for my response. "No?" I finally answered.

"Hopeless," she said, shaking her head. "Just hopeless."

I looked down at my feet and pretended to be studying the floorboards of the porch. By now both Aunt Elizabeth and my mother were shaking their heads.

"Go inside and get me an empty bottle from under the sink," Aunt Elizabeth said.

When I returned with the bottle, Aunt Elizabeth waved her hand toward the backyard. "Now go put a few bees in that thing."

I stood there. "What?"

"Make sure they are the stinging kind," she said. "I need the stinging kind."

"They all pretty much sting…"

"But not the males, right? The… what are they called?"

She seemed to know a little too much about this. "Drones."

"Right, the drones. None of them."

She must be reading *The ABC of Bee Culture* on the sly. "There aren't that many drones, anyway."

"Good, get me a jar of stinging females," she said.

"Now," said Mom.

I retreated to the backyard, where I saw Uncle Mike peeking from around his shed. He was looking for a report, but I just waved him off and walked over to the hive boxes. That sent him back into his shed, and I waited until I heard the shed door close before I lifted the top cover of the hive. I set the jar down, pulled out one of the comb frames, and in a quick, fluid motion, swept the bees from one corner of the comb into the open jar. I screwed the jar tight, slid the comb frame back into the hive, and covered the hive.

When I returned to the front porch, Mom was gone and Aunt Elizabeth was smoking her cigarette, looking across to the hearse as if contemplating her future in the reflection of the black chassis. I handed her the jar and stood there, wanting to say something.

"You're not going to…" I managed, before visions of Uncle Mike in agonizing and gruesome death prevented me from continuing.

She put her hand on my shoulder. "No, don't worry," she said with a smile, "I'm just going to practice."

Uncle Mike was as good as his word. When he promised not to use the hearse to cart around dead people, apparently, his promise didn't include stiffs.

At least that's what he called all the bodies he bought from the Waikīkī Wax Museum bankruptcy auction. I helped Uncle Mike unload the bodies, stacked like a cord of wood from floorboard to ceiling in the back of the hearse, in the middle of the night, about a week after getting the car.

"Don't lay them on the ground," he whispered to me. "They might get wet."

So we stood the wax figures up in the front yard: a trio of *haole* missionaries in black cassocks and wire-rimmed glasses, a couple of Chinese laborers fresh off the boat, some not unattractive topless Hawaiian maidens, a gang of drunken whalers with squinty expressions caught in mid jig, three of the Big Five Captains of Industry (Brewer, Davies, and Castle), a six-pack of swaddled royal babies (some moribund, some not), a random assortment of royal attendants and warriors complete with ceremonial capes and kahili standards, and even a couple of the lesser Kamehamehas, IV and V. It was sort of a motley crew, a collection of history's second-string players, and seeing them congregated like that in the moonlight inspired a gut-twisting pain and a sense of doom in me.

"Where's Kamehameha the Great or Liliuokalani?" I looked around the crowd that my shoeboxes of money had helped purchase. "I'd even settle for King Kalakaua."

"Most of the royals got bought up by other wax museums in private deals before the auction. Even the Smithsonian bought a couple," he explained. He gestured over to the Kamehamehas. "As it is, I was lucky to get Alexander Liholiho and Lot."

Uncle Mike walked over and put his arm over Lot's shoulder. "Howzit, braddahs," he said to them, making shakas and trying to get them to high-five. When he saw I wasn't laughing, he patted the stomach of Alexander Liholiho and said, "No wonder you died early. You need for eat, brah. What kind Hawaiian you?" Uncle Mike looked over at me again and sighed. "Tough audience," he said.

He walked over to the hearse and opened the passenger door. "I saved these two for last," he said as he ducked into the car.

Uncle Mike slid out the first stiff, and I grabbed it by its white shoes, followed by white pants and a white tunic jacket, and topped with a head of immaculately groomed white hair. "Duke," I said. "It's Duke Kahanamoku."

"Meet the Ambassador of Aloha," said Uncle Mike as he slipped a canoe paddle into his hand.

"Why is he holding that thing like a microphone? He looks like an idiot trying to speak into the handle of a paddle."

"I don't know, that's the way they had him at the museum," he said. "The tourists must have liked it that way."

Uncle Mike returned to the car and slid out another stiff in white shoes. As I helped him lift it out, I noticed that this one also had white pants and a white jacket, but the outfit was more fashionably extreme: an all-white tuxedo with orange pinstriping and flares in the bell bottoms and wrists that could hide a small dog. Uncle Mike stood him up and then looked at me. I shook my head. Then he slipped a microphone into the stiff's hand.

"Don Ho!" I said.

"The Ambassador of Waikīkī," said Uncle Mike.

"Mr. Aloha," I said.

"Hawaii's Ambassador of Love," said Uncle Mike.

We chuckled. I scooted Don next to Duke.

"He looks sort of short," I said.

"Yeah, but at least he's not drunk!"

We chuckled again. Uncle Mike looked Don and Duke over, carefully brushing off their immaculate white suits. "Had to pay a little extra to save these two."

"Save these two? Save them from what?"

"Who knows? Degradation, ridicule, mockery from some anti-establishment type," he said as he straightened the flaring collars of Don Ho's ruffled blouse. "There were a lot of shady characters at that auction."

I let the irony pass. Then a thought occurred to me. "If the wax museum in Waikīkī couldn't make money with all those tourists, then how are we going to?"

"That's a very good question," Uncle Mike said, starting to stroke his chin. "One that I have been thinking a lot about."

I could tell by the way he was pacing and the long silence he gave the question that he was thinking about it for the first time. "Well, I don't know, exactly," he said finally. "But I bought these on speculation… no, speculation is too strong a word, on…"

"Potential?"

"Yes, on potential. Because you know me," he slapped his chest. "When the opportunity presents itself, and it will, it always does. When it presents itself, I will not be like the hundreds or thousands of other men who pass it by unseeing, I will see it with my keen business eye for what it is and grab it! That you can bank your money on."

"I think I already have," I mumbled.

Uncle Mike ignored me. He started buffing Don and Duke's white shoes with the bottom of his shirt. He took his time about it, leaving me to ponder his business acumen. "Okay," he said finally, "Let's get them into your room."

"My room?"

"Yeah, I was thinking maybe you could move a few things and fit them into your closet…"

"What do you mean, my room? What's wrong with your house?"

"My house? The shed?" He looked at me with profound disappointment as if I had just given the wrong answer to the $64,000 question. Then he started poking me in the head with his finger. "Think, think! Even if there was room, these are from a wax museum, which means they are made of wax, and that shed gets really hot during the day…"

"…which melts the wax. Okay, I get it." I tried to think of some other solution, but like the hearse for my dates, I was once again stuck with an Uncle Mike solution. I picked up one of the topless wahines and carried her over my shoulder. "I better put this one in the closet before Mom sees it."

Getting them into my bedroom was no problem. Since he wasn't allowed in the house, Uncle Mike lined the stiffs outside the front door, and I just carried them over my shoulder into the bedroom like a fireman in reverse, rushing victims back into an unfortunate situation. In no time, almost all the denizens of the wax museum were off the lawn and gathered in my bedroom, waiting like impatient diners to be situated.

"Better lock your bedroom door," Uncle Mike whispered helpfully as he gave me the last one.

"Yeah, thanks," I said heavily, but Uncle Mike didn't hear me. He was already off the porch and on his way back to his shed.

After emptying my closet and throwing all the clothes under my bed, I stood two of the stiffs up at the ends of the closet and laid the rest of them down, stacking them precisely, fitting knobby elbows and knees into nooks and niches like how I imagined the wall of a log house was constructed. But even after I closed my bulging closet door, I was still left with about a dozen stiffs blocking every pathway in my bedroom. I needed at least a clear path to the bedroom door, so I lined them up like sentries next to my bed, discovering that one of them would have to share the bed with me if I wanted to open the door. Apprising my options, I disarmed Duke of his paddle and laid him on the bed since he was skinnier than Don. Despite having a cold, unfamiliar body next to me in bed and an audience standing over me like admiring stalkers, I somehow managed to fall asleep.

The next morning, Mom pounded on my bedroom door like she usually did to wake me up for school, but instead of opening the door and shouting her usual greeting, "You're late," all she could do was jiggle the knob.

"What is this," I heard her say from the other side of door. "Why is this locked?" I heard her rattle the doorknob again. "I don't like this."

I was sitting up in bed and wide awake by this time, trying to think of some reply, when I heard Aunt Elizabeth walk by the door in her high heels.

"It's his private social life," she said. "Evidently, he has one now."

"Ohhh," Mom said understandingly. She stopped trying the knob. "Well, your father... I mean, if he were here, bless his heart, he could talk to you..."

"Mom, no... that's not..."

"That's okay," she said, "You don't have to explain it to me."

I could hear Aunt Elizabeth snickering.

"No really, Mom, it's just..."

"No, I understand. It's normal. I just want you to know if you have any..."

"Issues," Aunt Elizabeth offered.

"Yes, or..."

"Questions," she offered again.

"Yes, then I want you to feel free to ask me," Mom said.

I buried my face in my hands.

"Or your Aunt Elizabeth," Aunt Elizabeth said.

"Okay?"

"Uncle Mike..." I began, as I tried to explain one more time.

"Yes, he's okay as well," Mom said.

I gave up and lay back down. "Okay."

"Good," Mom said. "I'm going to leave now." I heard her pad her way into the kitchen. There was a moment of silence and then Aunt Elizabeth said softly on the other side of the door, "We know what you're doing in there."

I looked over at Duke. "I wish," I told him.

While Uncle Mike spent his days driving the hearse around with his "keen business eye" looking for his "opportunity," Aunt Elizabeth was storming around the island on bus, practicing her stinging. At first, she stung old Chinese ladies, immigrants from the turn of the century, who referred each other to her for help with their arthritis or rheumatism. With as many as a dozen stings per hand, hip, elbow, knee, or shoulder, Aunt Elizabeth was able to relieve not only the pain, but restore litheness to their joints and allow these matriarchs to assume command of their kitchens once again for weddings and birthday feasts done in the proper old style. Such miracles did not come without reward—monetary and otherwise—and so Aunt Elizabeth was often invited to these celebrations, where she went toting her bees. She had designed a special carrying cage for her work, one that looked secure enough to calm the bus drivers yet was hinged and compartmentalized to give her quick and easy access to one bee at a time. She had given me a hundred dollars and a drawing of her design to build, but I kept the money and passed the task onto Uncle Mike, knowing that he would be grateful for any chance to serve his beloved. Master prison handicrafter that he was, Uncle Mike produced a stunning koa-wood and gold-net creation that Aunt Elizabeth filled with bees and carried off with her every night for her sessions, while Uncle Mike pined from the shed window and wished that the handle of the cage was his hand.

As much as I hated to admit it, Uncle Mike turned out to be right about Sara. After a few weeks of enduring eye jokes and crude innuendos from my peers— weeks where I studiously avoided any eye contact with Sara at all, not to lessen my pain but to keep the wolves from attacking her—things calmed down and subtle changes started taking place. At first, they just confused me: Was she really turned toward me a little more in class? Did she really just uncross and recross her legs when I happened to glance over? Were her friends really nudging each other when I passed them in the halls? But as time went on, and I got less covert and bolder in my longing, I noticed that Sara's eyelid seemed to flutter more when she knew I was looking at her, which I interpreted as the involuntary reflex of the passions hidden in her own heart. Then one day when she ended up behind me as I finished at the water fountain, red-faced, eye atwitter like the wing of a hummingbird, a press of grinning friends behind her blocking her escape, I knew that soon, really soon, I would have my opportunity.

Unfortunately, Uncle Mike's opportunity arrived first, and like most of his business dealings, it came in a hurry. Near midnight one Friday night, he woke me with a rendition of "Taps" blaring from the new car horn he had installed in the hearse. Mom, Aunt Elizabeth, and practically everyone else on the lane were yelling obscenities by the time I stumbled out onto the porch in my pajamas, and all I could do was curse like the rest of them and try to hold back Uncle Mike, who had burst out of the car and bounded up the steps to wave his arms and point with his hands while he shouted in my face, none of which I heard until the horn finally completed its mournful dirge.

"...leave now!" he finished.

He stood there with an expectant look on his face, like an eager Boy Scout who had just completed a good deed and was waiting for an acknowledgment. "I can't believe I gave you a hundred dollars to buy that stupid noisy horn," I said.

"What?" Uncle Mike looked back briefly at the car. "If you think it's loud out here, you should hear it inside the car." I groaned. Uncle Mike then waved at the neighbors who appeared in various forms of undress in their doorways and windows. Most of them gave him the one-finger salute back. "Anyway, forget the horn! What do you think about the debut?"

"Debut? What debut?"

Uncle Mike shook his head. "Haven't you been listening to anything I've said? For the guys!"

"The guys? You mean the Duke and the Don?"

"No, no, no," he said. "I mean all the guys! Never mind, we just got to go. We'll spiff them up when we get there. Let's load up!"

He spun me around and pushed me back into the house where I dutifully started retrieving the stiffs. First my bed buddy, Duke, then the gaggle of standing admirers, followed by the denizens of the closet, all the while changing out of my pajamas between trips, a piece at a time. By the time I was fully clothed, Uncle Mike had packed the stiffs into the hearse and was only waiting for the babies that I had carried out in a grocery sack.

"I had a hard time finding the last two," I said, as I handed him the bag. "I forgot I ran out of room in the dresser drawers and ended up putting two of them in my desk."

"That's okay, we only really need them for packing anyway," he said as he took the babies out and wedged them among the feet of the stacked stiffs. "We don't want these guys to roll around."

After packing the stiffs as tight as the Tokyo subway, Uncle Mike threw me the keys and went around to the passenger's side. "You drive. We have to go to Maunakea Street to pick up some red carnation *lei* for Duke and Don first," he said. "Everyone will be expecting them to have one."

I started up the hearse and was letting it rumble to life when I glanced back at the house. There was Aunt Elizabeth watching us from the window, scorn and disdain emanating from her backlit silhouette. An instinct to flee seized my foot and I gunned the accelerator, lurching us away from the curb with a loud farting backfire and sailing out of the lane as I aimed toward Chinatown.

I learned that the only people in Chinatown at that time of the night were the dead, the horny, and the people who serviced them. The hookers gave the hearse a wide berth when we pulled up to one of the twenty-four-hour *lei* stands, and Uncle Mike took so long haggling with the *lei* seller about a pair of day-old red carnation *lei* that I was terrified one of the girls would come over and yell at me for ruining business or worse yet, try to interest me while I waited in the car. My previous experience with hookers had been limited to harassing them while they were arm-in-arm with an aged tourist or Japanese businessman as some friends and I cruised Waikīkī from the safety of a moving car. Uncle Mike took so long that a few of the younger girls did wander over to peer in the car, but I kept my window rolled up and looked straight ahead like some kind of puritanical zealot, which sent the girls laughing back to the group. I strained to keep myself in this position until Uncle Mike returned to the car.

Having gotten the *lei*, Uncle Mike had me drive a little ways further then pull onto a side street, where I had to stop behind some vans that were blocking the street while they unloaded tables, chairs, and catering equipment.

"It looks like a party," I said.

"It is," said Uncle Mike. "The best kind of party, a Chinese funeral." He pointed to a sign on the building in front of us: Deliveries Only—Mililani Mortuary. "I'm going in there, you start unloading the stiffs."

"What? Here?"

"What did you think? You can't have a party without entertainment."

"We're the entertainment? At a funeral?"

"True, we're not the big show," he admitted. And then to reassure me, he patted my arm. "We're more like an opening act."

I was speechless. Uncle Mike took the opportunity to remind me to clean the white shoes of the entertainers, fluff up the feather capes of the warriors and royalty, and make sure that none of the topless native maidens had bad bed hair. Then he left and disappeared inside the building, leaving me to unload the stiffs and line them up next to the car like a costumed chorus line, while deliverymen, loaders, and caterers gave me curious glances.

It was a nine a.m. funeral for the patriarch of the Chun Hoon family, founder of one of Hawaii's earliest and most famous supermarkets, and assured to be well attended by the island elite. We worked through the night, cleaning and adjusting the stiffs, deciding which could be used solo and which would have to be grouped, and then spent most of the early morning deciding the most crucial factor, placement. At the formal entrance to the mortuary, we secured a front-door location for Don Ho (since he was part Chinese), using him to prop open one of the doors and welcome visitors with his hit "I'll Remember You" playing on continuous loop on a tape recorder hidden in his flaring bell bottoms. Kamehameha IV and V were placed at the end of a reception line where the family would line up to receive mourners. Kahili standard bearers and an assortment of nobles in attendance were arranged on a dais behind the open casket. With a couple of borrowed uniforms from the caterers, we shirted the topless maidens and stationed them behind the steam table for the hot foods and hoped they wouldn't melt. We set most of the warriors on the sidewalk outside the mortuary to entice visitors off the street. By show time, we were left with only Duke Kahanamoku, which we didn't want to return to the car like the nineteenth-century missionaries and the Chinese laborers, which we had thought about using but later rejected as possibly being misconstrued as a mocking comment on the Chun Hoon family's humble beginnings. Duke really had no place at the funeral, but his instant recognizability would be sure to delight, and besides, we had already invested in a *lei* for him. We carried Duke around inside and outside the mortuary, trying to locate a good spot for him, but nothing seemed to work. Uncle Mike wanted Duke to be more than a potted plant in the background and yet did not want people to line up to see a wax curiosity, which would detract from the main event, the dead guy in the coffin. We were still running Duke around when the family and the first mourners arrived, and maybe the stress of that combined with the numerous cups of coffee I had begged off the caterers all night suddenly seized my bladder, and I needed to find a bathroom. Immediately. Leaving Duke outside the restroom, I went inside and sought my relief. When I came back out, it hit me that Duke was exactly where he needed to be, so after Uncle Mike unscrewed the restrooms sign from the wall, I taped it to the blade of Duke's paddle and twisted it in his hand so it looked as if Duke was pointing the way to the restrooms with his paddle.

The funeral was a bigger hit than we and the Chun Hoon family had anticipated. Tourists in Chinatown and locals on errands were drawn off the street by their curiosity about the stiffs and ended up giving bereavement money to the family. At the height of the funeral, based on the number of inappropriately dressed impromptu mourners, we calculated at least a thirty-five percent increase over the planned amount.

"That kind of traffic," my uncle said to me after I calculated the numbers, "is money in the bank."

And he was right. That evening we collected our flat fee plus a percentage on the take as a bonus from the Chun Hoon family, and in no time, the word was out. From our first couple of gigs, Uncle Mike was able to get the black hearse repainted in a navy blue with the name of his business emblazoned on the sides: CELEBRITY STIFFS, ESCORTS TO THE AFTERLIFE, ROYAL—HISTORICAL—ENTERTAINMENT. After a profile in the business section of the newspaper called "Dawn of the Dead" that chronicled Uncle Mike's shrewd entrepreneurial eye in this new market, business really exploded, and we were even busier than during Uncle Mike's fraudulent *nakahodo* days. Funerals were much more lucrative because, while weddings had to be scheduled on weekends due to people's reluctance to miss work for love, the stronger emotions of guilt, fear, and regret drove people to funerals even during the weekdays.

We could accommodate almost any request. For one funeral, we converted a whaler into Tom Selleck by buying the stiff a curly wig, trimming his moustache, slapping a baseball cap upon his head, and decking him out in an aloha shirt, Bermuda shorts, and shoes (no socks) in true *haole* fashion. The final touch was a pair of large aviator sunglasses that hid his features. Suddenly, there he was, Magnum P.I., standing in front of us. We had kits to convert a missionary into the Pope for especially pious funerals, and we even had plans to turn our most rejected figure, Sanford B. Dole, Hawaii's first governor by virtue of leading the rebellion that overthrew the monarchy, into a Santa Claus for the holiday funerals, thanks to Dole's ridiculously long white beard.

Meanwhile, Aunt Elizabeth had expanded her practice from just rheumatic Chinese ladies to people of all races and ailments, offering relief for conditions as diverse as sciatica, migraine, loss of appetite, and even severe cases of acne and eczema. We were getting so many calls at all times of the day and night for "The Bee Lady of Nu'uanu" that we stopped answering the phone and let Aunt Elizabeth pick up with her new greeting, "Bees!" Her big break came when she cured the bad back of a mailman who had been on disability for over ten years. After two applications and nearly a hundred bee carcasses, he returned to work to greet shocked coworkers and resume his route. Once she got plugged into the postal service network and their inexhaustible supply of bad backs, bum knees, turned ankles, and strained wrists, she knew she could quit her day job.

But the biggest change and the most welcome one to both Uncle Mike and myself was when Aunt Elizabeth asked me to move the hives to the front of the house ostensibly so she could take care of them herself. She needed to keep better track of her inventory, she told me, but as I told Uncle Mike, "She could have taken care of them back here, too. I think she may have other reasons."

He just smiled and bided his time, "accidentally" showing up at the right moment to help her carry some new hive boxes, or "luckily" going in the same direction as Aunt Elizabeth's next appointment so that she wouldn't have to take the bus.

As for me, I was just grateful to be rid of the responsibilities for the bees, because even the little I needed to do was too much for our busy funeral schedule. When I booked funerals, I offered the families a discount if they announced in the obituaries that Celebrity Stiffs would be at the funeral. They nearly always accepted, and our performances became something like the social hits of the season. People shopped the obituaries like they shopped the movie schedules and planned their entertainment around our events. I saw many repeat funeral-goers, especially kids from school, and the stature of being involved with Uncle Mike's business, even though I was just the secretary/chauffeur/stevedore, lent me an aura of social prestige that I never could have attained otherwise. In spite of my new "cool" status, I refrained from indulging in the benefits of my new social position except once. It was nearing the end of prom ticket sales time and I had been inundated with silent beseeching looks from Sara's friends in the hallways for weeks. Even Sara had grown suddenly demure around me, looking down whenever I looked at her so that her drooping eyelid drooped even lower, like she was indifferent to the attention she was receiving and was giving her hangnails profound concentration. I chose to trap her in the hallway after school when she was with all of her friends, so that the entire school would know. As I expected, Sara turned shyly away from me when I approached her group.

"Sara, if it's not too late," I said to her back while her friends shuffled behind her like an emotional backstop, "I'd like to take you to the prom."

Sara turned in a dramatic fashion, and with only the faintest stirring of a smile nodded once. But she couldn't control the excitement of her eyelid which was stuttering, "Yes, oh, yes."

Pride surged in me and I told her, "Great, I'll pick you up," before starting to walk away. I let myself get some distance before turning back to her by swiveling my upper body in runway model fashion, and saying proudly, "Oh, by the way, we'll be going in the hearse."

Sara turned around to her conspiracy of friends, and they all huddled around her and giggled.

The day of the prom also happened to be a good day for funerals. We had several gigs that day, and for pre-prom entertainment, I had the choice of taking Sara to the viewing of the matriarch of a prominent Hawaiian family where the food promised to be plentiful and authentic, or the services for the colorful Waikīkī entrepreneur, Dodo Sands. I decided on the Dodo Sands event, not only because the real, non-stiff Don Ho was likely to be there (having gotten his first big break from Dodo by performing in the Sandcastle Restaurant) but mainly because we were still a one-car family and Uncle Mike needed to take Aunt Elizabeth to that funeral.

She had finally relented, agreeing to attend one of Uncle Mike's productions for the purpose, as he put it, of cross-marketing. "A chance to relieve the pain and suffering of those until they become my clients," he told her. He finally closed the deal by telling her that at Dodo Sand's funeral, there would be many members of the Hawaiian Musicians and Entertainers Union, where many a hula dancer's sore feet and a musician's stiff hands could be found.

So it was a family affair when we pulled up to Sara's house in the hearse, Aunt Elizabeth up front with her travel case full of bees, Uncle Mike in the driver's seat with a chauffeur's cap he bought especially for the occasion.

"Remember," he told me before I got out of the car, "when I'm wearing the hat, I'm no longer your Uncle Mike. I'm just some guy you hired to drive the car."

"Yeah," said Aunt Elizabeth, "Just another ex-con."

Uncle Mike smiled at her. "An ex-con trying to go straight."

"Whatevahs," she said. "Be sure to call him 'boy.'"

"Or brah," he said. "Like, 'Ey, brah, go drop us off before parking the car.'"

I just shook my head and escaped from the car with the corsage. In proper ladylike fashion, Sara made me wait in the living room with her anxious parents, who eyed me suspiciously. None of us said a word while the minutes ticked by, and the place started to feel like a meeting between historical enemies. Having no peace offering, I tried to relieve the tension by sliding the corsage across the coffee table. To my surprise, Sara's dad grabbed it and held it up, examining it closely.

"This didn't come from some dead lady's funeral, did it?" he asked.

"Oh, no. No, of course not."

His wife hit him in the shoulder. "What?" he said to her, as she took the corsage away from him and handed it back to me, "I gotta ask don't I?"

"No, we take an oath," I explained.

"An oath?"

"Yes, an oath to secrecy." I thought for a moment. "To neither displace any matériel nor divulge the intimate details of the events we participate in."

"Like a priest in confession?" Sara's dad asked.

"Yeah, sort of like that. Although we think of it more like the privilege between an attorney and client, or doctor and patient."

"Let's hear the oath," he said.

Sara's dad was impressed, you could tell, but his wife hit him in the shoulder again, and so he shut up with kind of a disappointed look on his face. Luckily, Sara made her entrance soon after and everything was forgotten in a flurry of picture-taking of the usual sort: girl and date standing in the living room, girl and parents, girl by herself, girl being pinned with the corsage, another picture of newly corsaged girl and date; and once we got out of the house, a repeat of same except next to the car.

When we pulled away from the curb, I was about to introduce Sara to Uncle Mike and Aunt Elizabeth, but Uncle Mike said, "Shall I put up the privacy screen, sir?"

"We have a privacy screen?"

"Of course, sir, it just needed a repair." He punched a button and a smoky glass window rose from behind the front bench seats.

"The last time I heard you speak that politely was in the courthouse," Aunt Elizabeth said.

"Yeah, I almost said, 'Your Honor,'" Uncle Mike said before the screen closed him off.

Suddenly, Sara and I were alone, and I struggled to think of some witty banter. But the only thing I could come up with was the pedestrian "I hear the caterers will be from the dead guy's restaurant."

Sara just nodded and looked around.

"The Sandcastle, I think it's called. They're supposed to have really good ribs…" I felt like an idiot. I looked away from Sara and through the smoked-glass screen. I could just make out the silhouettes of Uncle Mike and Aunt Elizabeth nodding their heads and laughing. I watched him try and put his arm over her shoulder and her pushing him off three times, before she allowed him to rest it on the seat back behind her.

"Yes," Sara said and continued to look around until she spotted the long hearse bed behind her where we usually loaded the stiffs. "Is this where…"

I nodded. "I like your dress," I said suddenly. I really did. It was a blue off-the-shoulder kind of thing that left her whole left shoulder and upper arm bare, which lent a nakedness to that side and emphasized the heavily painted eyelid and fake eyelashes of her bewitching eye.

She looked at me and smiled. It was then that she had a look on her face I had never seen before, her glittering eyelids languidly hanging about her face, beckoning me like lingerie hung from one finger before it silently slips to the floor. "Sit here," she said as she patted the bench seat next to her.

I dutifully obeyed and whispered, "I've never made out in a hearse before."

Sara just smiled and sometime in the silent happiness on the way to the mortuary, I slipped my hand into hers.

ACKNOWLEDGMENTS

I would like to gratefully acknowledge the publications in which these stories previously appeared:

"Christmas Stories," "The Summer of Miracles and Lies,"
"Relievers" —*Bamboo Ridge*
"The Shadow Artist" —*North American Review*
"Trading Heroes" —*Sonora Review*
"The Icebox Stay Coming," "Wooing Elizabeth" —*Zyzzyva*

The stories in this collection are a lifetime's work, but it wasn't an effort I bore alone.

Many thanks to my first reader, peerless editor, narrative diagnostician, and sister, Marli Higa. You always know what I'm trying to write even when I don't always get there. I'm also indebted to David Carkeet, who nurtured my early work and remains my inspiration, model, and guide to the literary life.

Many thanks to those who took my work seriously, even when I wasn't sure:

Eric Chock and Darrell H.Y. Lum of *Bamboo Ridge*
Howard Junker of *Zyzzyva*

Profs. Ed Hackett, Alan Nadel, Valerie Miner, and Ron Carlson
My ASU creative writing cohort, especially Rick Noguchi, Deneen Jenks, and
Steve Scafidi
Janet Y. Jackson and Iris Csik of the St. Louis writers' group
The Kaimuki Writers' Workshop

To Jenny Molberg and the staff at Pleiades Press: Every moment working with
you has been a joy. Thank you for making my dream come true.

Finally, to my parents, James and June Higa, who taught me the value of community and home, *mahalo* for the sacrifices you made for me. And many thanks
to my wife Marguerite, whose fierce love is my foundation and protection and
the only reason I've been able to get this far.

ABOUT THE AUTHOR

Jeffrey J. Higa is the great-grandson of Okinawan and Japanese immigrants who came to Hawaii at the turn of the 20th century to work on the sugar plantations. From them, he inherited their love of their adopted land and the stories that sustained them. He left Hawaii soon after high school to attend Rensselaer Polytechnic Institute in Troy, New York, where he graduated with a bachelor's of science degree. However, it was his experience living above a used bookstore in downtown Troy, where paperbacks could be bought for a quarter, that launched his interest in writing. During his graduate education, Jeffrey taught, wrote, and worked with indigenous youth to tell their stories as he wandered through several writing programs until finally finding a home at the University of Missouri–St. Louis where he finished with a M.A. in creative writing. Since then, his play *Futless* won the Hawai'i Prize from the Kumu Kahua Theatre and "Christmas Stories" was serialized and broadcast by Aloha Shorts on Hawaii Public Radio. His story "The Shadow Artist" received an honorable mention in the Kurt Vonnegut Speculative Fiction Prize from the North American Review. He currently lives in Honolulu with his wife, the biologist Marguerite Butler, his daughter, the poet and actor Raine Higa, and their good dog Tim Tam. *Calabash Stories* is his first short story collection.

THE ROBERT C. JONES PRIZE
FOR SHORT PROSE

Robert C. Jones was a professor of English at the University of Central Missouri and an editor at Mid-American Press who supported and encouraged countless young writers throughout a lifetime of editing and teaching. His legacy continues to inspire all of us who live, write, and support the arts in mid-America.

The editors at Pleiades Press select 10-15 finalists from among those manuscripts submitted each year. A judge of national renown selects one winner for publication.

ALSO AVAILABLE FROM PLEIADES PRESS

The Cipher by Molly Brodak
Geographic Tongue by Rodney Gomez
dark // thing by Ashley M. Jones
The Olive Trees' Jazz and Other Poems by Samira Negrouche,
    translated by Marilyn Hacker
Louder Birds by Angela Voras-Hills
Miracles Come on Mondays by Penelope Cray
The Imaginary Age by Leanna Petronella
Fluid States by Heidi Czerwiec
A Lesser Love by E. J. Koh
Destruction of the Lover by Luis Panini, translated by Lawrence Schimel
How to Tell if You are Human: Diagram Poems by Jessy Randall
Bridled by Amy Meng
30 Questions People Don't Ask: The Selected Poems of Inga Gaile,
    translated by Ieva Lešinka
The Darkness Call by Gary Fincke
In Between: Poetry Comics by Mita Mahato
Novena by Jacques J. Rancourt
Book of No Ledge: Visual Poems by Nance Van Winckel
Landscape with Headless Mama by Jennifer Ghivan